THE CLASS VILLAIN

Coral Elizabeth and Katherine Lee

THE CLASS VILLAIN
Coral Elizabeth and Katherine Lee

ISBN: 9781982954314

Dedicated to:

My parents, my Space Parents, and all those who have supported me in becoming an author.

      -Katherine Lee

To my family for always being amazing and supportive- I would even go so far as to say you've been...SUPER.

      -Coral Elizabeth

Part One:

Heroes

CHAPTER ONE

Gloria sat on the floor of her bedroom, her chemistry notes spread out to one side. On her other side, her card tower was reaching impressive heights. She chewed her lip absently as she tried to remember her notes and stack another card at the same time. Chemistry was a distracting subject, chemical reactions and processes always ended up making her think about superpowers.

Then again, lately everything made her think about superpowers. She was twelve, shouldn't she have hers by now? Both her parents did, even her older sister, Victoria, had them. Her card tower crumbled as her train of thought slid from the tracks.

Gloria sighed and turned back to her notes when she heard her mother calling from the kitchen.

"Gloria! Vicky! Breakfast!" her mother's voice rang out, and Gloria scrambled to get up. She slipped on the cards and crashed back to the floor.

"Coming!" Gloria shouted, pulling herself up with the doorknob. She was met with the smell of warm oatmeal wafting up from the kitchen.

"How'd it go last night?" Gloria asked.

"It went well," said her mom. Her silver gloves and cape were currently disconnected from the rest of her uniform and set aside on an empty stool, replaced instead by a denim apron. A pan full of scrambled eggs sizzled faintly on the stovetop while she pulled plates out of the cupboard. "We found the technopath who was hacking the grid and, well, froze his assets." She grinned and Gloria rolled her eyes. "He's in a secure cell now. Do you want some eggs?"

"Sure," Gloria said. She got a plate and started piling eggs onto it. Her mom had ice powers, Victoria, or Vicky, as she went by now, had storm

1

powers, and what could Gloria do? Math. "Hey, do you think it's possible to get your powers and not know it?"

"Hm, I suppose it's possible," said her mom, "but I've never heard of it happening. Powers have a tendency to sort of announce their arrival, you know? Like when Vicky got hers." Her older sister Vicky had, according to her mother, thrown a tantrum in her high chair and made it rain inside the kitchen. "But you really shouldn't stress about it; lots of heroes started out as late bloomers."

This wasn't exactly helpful. She was already late enough. When were her powers coming?

"I guess, yeah," Gloria said with a sigh. "But isn't this a little...extra late?"

"You know, when a child is born from parents without powers," said her mom, chilling a glass of orange juice before setting it on the counter, "their powers often don't come until they get into their teens. While it's rarer, that can happen in families with powered parents, too. Yours could come any time in the next few years or so and it wouldn't be any stretch to reality. Right now, you should be focusing more on your schoolwork."

Gloria groaned. She couldn't wait years, she had already waited twelve! She wasn't supposed to have to wait that long at all; she had two super parents. Maybe that meant she didn't even have powers. No, she didn't want to think about that. Better to talk about grades any day.

"My grades are fine," Gloria said, pushing her eggs around on their plate.

"Well, you could also work on making some new friends." Her mom pushed forward a glass of juice. "Is there anyone at school you'd like to invite over to study with sometime?"

"You could always invite Derek," said Vicky with a sly smile, coming down the stairs. Vicky was only here for a week for her school break from college, but that didn't stop her from poking her nose in Gloria's business in what time she had.

"No," Gloria said flatly. "He's a creep." Derek had his own superpowers, but they were freaky. He could control shadows and mostly used it to antagonize the other super-powered kids at school. So far, that didn't include Gloria.

"I don't really know anyone well enough to invite them over," Gloria said with a shrug, looking back down at her plate. Her best friend Amber had moved away over the summer. Since then, Gloria hadn't been able to find a new group she fit in with. Just thinking about introducing herself and talking to people was nerve-wracking enough, she could hardly imagine actually doing it.

Her mom gave a somewhat disappointed "hm," as she set up another plate of eggs. "Well, maybe Vicky can help you study for that Chemistry test you have coming up. Isn't that this week?"

"It's not until Friday," Gloria said. "And I've got most of the material memorized."

Gloria hoped Vicky would say she was busy. It wasn't that Vicky was mean, really, she was just….Vicky. The smart one, the pretty one, the one that wasn't a huge disappointment for having no powers and no friends. Being around her too much was just exhausting.

"Including all of the formulas?" said her mom. "You won't be ready for the test until you have those and the vocabulary words from this unit down pat. Don't forget, anyone can be born with superpowers, but only hard workers become heroes." Behind their mother, Vicky mouthed the words as their mom said them. They both had that saying memorized.

"Uh oh, check out the time," said Vicky, nodding at the clock on the stove. "Better eat quick, Gloria, or you'll be late."

Gloria shoved the remaining scrambled eggs into her mouth and raced up the stairs. She stuffed her chemistry notes in her backpack, swiftly zipping it closed.

"Bye, mom!" she called as she ran out the door. She stuffed her backpack in her bike basket and took off towards the school.

She picked up speed as the school came into view, zooming down the last hill. She was only a block away when she swerved with a cry of alarm, a car pulling in front of her as she crossed the street. She was going too fast, and she could feel the tires slipping out from under her.

Gloria closed her eyes and heard a terrible crunching sound as her bike went under the car. But….Gloria herself didn't even land for a few more seconds, and when she did it was on grass. She opened her eyes, looking around in confusion. She was covered in grainy dust, almost like sand, and several yards away from where her bike now lay. One wheel was bent nearly at ninety degrees, making a pathetic attempt to spin.

"What….?" Gloria said aloud, standing. As she tried to shake off some of the dust, a sudden gust of wind nearly knocked her over. Gloria looked down at her hands. Could it be?

She thrust out her hands in front of her, and the grass bent over as a burst of wind flew around her. There was a rushed tickling sensation through her arms, just beneath the skin.. A balloon swelled inside her chest, then popped in an explosion of joy.

Gloria laughed gleefully, jumping in the air until she heard the school bell ringing. Her eyes widened. School.

She only had five minutes before she had to be in class. Gloria quickly picked up her bike, told the rather surprised driver she was fine and ran towards the school. Her bike scraped along behind her until she dumped it at a bike rack and ran to class.

She made it, just barely, and took her seat. It was almost impossible to pay attention. All Gloria wanted to do was test out her new powers, and, of course, today was Wednesday, which meant the Super-Club would be meeting after school. Nobody could get in unless they had superpowers. They were the future superheroes of the school and the most popular kids. Now, Gloria thought with a small smile, she would finally be one of them.

CHAPTER TWO

The club met in one of the larger classrooms, and the door was guarded, as it always was, by Mori Sang and one of the copies he was able to make of himself. Rumor had it that he could make up to thirteen total copies, though right now there were just the two of him. Regular club members like Emilia Mark and Janelle Ingersoll passed him without a problem. When Gloria tried to enter, however, a third duplicate of Mori appeared directly in the doorway.

"Hey, powers only," he said. "You got one?"

"Oh, yeah," Gloria said nervously, her stomach immediately turning in a panicked dance. What if they didn't believe her? Or what if her powers stopped working after this morning?

"Well, can I see it?" said Mori. The three of him crossed their arms. Gloria nodded and looked down at her hands.

"Yeah....uh, hang on a sec," she stammered. "I'm still getting used to it...." She tried to remember how she had done it that morning, then pushed her hand forward. The gust of wind was stronger than she had meant, and nearly knocked one of the Mori's off his feet.

"Sorry!" Gloria said quickly. "It wasn't supposed to be that big...."

"Don't worry about it," said Mori, grinning. His third duplicate disappeared with a pop, and the other two gestured for her to enter. "Welcome to the club. What's your name?"

"Gloria," she said with a quick smile, heading into the classroom. "Gloria Amari. Thanks."

Inside, there were already eight students assembled, sitting and talking amongst each other. She recognized many of them from around school and the stories told by other students. There was Emilia, of course, a very pretty but very aggressive girl with blonde hair, blue eyes, and the ability

5

to turn into a human bonfire. Janelle, a shy girl, hidden behind a veil of straight brown hair. Gloria had seen her with club members but didn't know her power.

Then there was Scuba, a lanky boy with a comically dramatic cowlick on the side of his head; she shared a few classes with him. She was pretty sure his real name was Spencer, but he used his bubble powers to breathe underwater during a field trip to the pool once. He'd made a large bubble over his head like a diving helmet, proclaimed himself to be the "scuba master," and had never shed the nickname.

There was also a girl who could make force fields, and a boy with telekinesis, but she didn't remember their names, and she couldn't remember much at all about the other students.

Maybe trying to get to know them before now would have been a good idea. It was too late for that now, though, so Gloria found a seat with a group of them and took it. She tried to think of something to say, but came up short and just tried not to look awkward holding her backpack.

Emilia glanced at her. "Hey," she said, looking somewhat confused. She didn't recognize Gloria. "Are you new?"

"Yeah," Gloria said with a nod. "I just got my powers this morning."

"Cool, what can you do?" Emilia asked.

"Wind, so far," Gloria said, glancing down at her hands.

"So kinda like Scuba, huh?" said Emilia. "Well, then you can join my team. I already told Scuba I'm going to be part of an all-girls superhero team. I don't want any dumb guys slowing me down." She stuck her tongue out at Scuba.

Scuba circled his fingers about his lips and blew a large, soapy bubble, which floated over and attached to Emilia's nose. "Whatever. I'll be on an even cooler team."

Emilia irritably popped the bubble with a swat of her hand. "Colder, maybe." She turned back to Gloria. "You are planning on being a superhero, right? I mean, this club is just for future heroes, there are some kids who just want to be superpowered civilians. Well, besides Derek, he says he's going to be a supervillain, so he's not allowed to join."

"Why's he want to be a supervillain, anyway?" said Gloria. "Being a hero is so much better."

Emilia shrugged. "Maybe some people are just wired different, you know? I mean, it could be his powers or something. He can attack people with shadows; it's creepy. He hasn't attacked anybody yet, but he did steal my pencils out of my backpack with it."

"He is pretty creepy," Gloria agreed.

Emilia leaned back in her chair and flipped her hair over her shoulder. "I'm not too worried, though. It just means I already know one of the people I'll be taking down when I'm a hero."

Mori came into the room, letting his duplicate disappear.

"Okay, so we've got two options for today," he said. "I've got some hero movies we could watch and, you know, talk about or something, or we could do study groups like last time. I mean, I've got a chemistry test coming up, so I'll technically be studying either way."

Everyone muttered quietly, then slowly people popped up with a vote for one side or the other. As the vote swayed toward studying, Scuba moaned loudly.

"Why do we only do boring stuff?" he complained.

"Because Mori's in charge," said Emilia with a shrug. "And, you know, we do have tests."

A general murmur of agreement to both statements sounded in the group, and everyone split off to study for their respective subjects.

Gloria slid her backpack to the ground and pulled out her Chemistry binder. Mori recognized some of the class handouts she took out and approached her.

"Hey, are we in the same class?" he asked.

"Oh, do you have Mrs. Welch?" Gloria asked. "You might be in a different period."

"Right, probably," said Mori. "Well, you can come join my group if you want. We're studying for the test on Friday."

"Thanks," Gloria said with a small smile, getting up to sit with his group. "I just need to finish memorizing some equations, I think...."

"The test is mostly going to focus on the unit conversions in the metric system," said Janelle. She was already seated with the group by where Mori's stuff was. "There won't be any questions on the other formulas until we go more in depth on them next unit."

"Oh," Gloria said hesitantly. "Um, are you sure?"

"She's a psychic," said Mori. "She always knows what to study for the tests."

"Woah," Gloria said, looking over at Janelle. "That's so cool." And it was a relief that she wouldn't need the formulas memorized by Friday.

"Yeah, cool," said Mori, "but she never tells me what grade I'm going to get."

Janelle gave a small, knowing smile. "If I did that, you wouldn't study, then you wouldn't get the grade." She looked at Gloria. "We're in the same class, right? I sit in the back, to the left of you."

"Um, yeah," Gloria said. "I'm Gloria. Oh....you already know that...."

Janelle smiled. "That's alright," she said. "Do you have the conversions in your notes?"

"Yep," Gloria said, opening her binder and flicking through the pages. "Right....here."

"Great, pass it here and I'll tell you units to convert, then you and Mori can race to see who answers first," said Janelle. "Winner gets to the make the questions next round."

"Alright." Gloria rubbed her hands together and looked over at Mori, "Game on."

The next day, as Gloria entered the school, she was disappointed to find she felt about the same. It didn't make sense, everything was supposed to be different now, wasn't it? However, she drifted to the corner of the lunchroom to eat by herself. Other than going to the club, she wasn't sure what was supposed to be different. She got a few glances from passing students, but other than that...

Mori came to sit by her. "Hey, Gloria," he said. "What are you doing all the way over here?"

"Oh, um, this is where I usually eat," Gloria said, surprised.

"Huh," said Mori. He looked around. "Seems a bit remote."

"You should come sit with us," Scuba said as he passed.

"Oh," Gloria said. "Um, sure." She smiled. Maybe not everything was the same.

Mori picked up his tray and made a double to carry hers. "Here, let me help."

"Thanks," Gloria said. She handed the tray to the double and followed them.

They sat at a table further into the cafeteria. Emilia was already sitting there with Janelle.

"There you guys are," said Emilia. "I was going to start looking for you. This is still the usual spot, right?"

"Yeah," said Mori. "We just had to get Gloria first."

Emilia nodded, looking at Gloria. Gloria sat down and tried to ignore the army of caterpillars crawling around in her stomach. She reminded herself that she had superpowers now, of course she belonged here. Gloria nibbled her sandwich. She usually just studied or something during lunch. There was no way she would be doing that now. Now she had people to talk to.

"So, I set fire to some drapes yesterday," said Emilia. She grinned, sounding rather proud of it.

Mori laughed. "New ones or the same ones?"

"New ones, in the kitchen this time," said Emilia. She looked at Gloria. "This is the third time I've done that. Apparently, I'm something of a fire hazard at home."

"Sounds kind of dangerous," Gloria said. She took another bite of sandwich, chewing slowly. She didn't have any cool stories she could tell about her powers yet. But her powers were just air, would she ever have a cool story like Emilia's?

"Eh, yeah, but we keep fire extinguishers in just about every room," said Emilia. "My dad has the same powers as me, and my mom makes force fields."

"Oh hey, Gloria," said Mori. "Is your mom joining my parent's team? My parents said something about a Mrs. Amari yesterday."

"Oh, I haven't heard." Gloria shrugged. Great, now she was even behind on news about their parents. How did they all know? All her mom wanted to do was make ice puns and ask about her grades, usually. "I'll have to ask her about it."

"That'd be pretty cool," Scuba said. He tossed a grape in the air and opened his mouth to catch it. It hit him in the eye, and across the table Emilia snorted.

Gloria nodded. "Yeah."

"I hear your dad is pretty cool," said Janelle. "He works with the FBI a lot, right? I've been considering working with something like that."

"Yeah, he helps them with investigations and stuff," Gloria said. Her dad could read minds. While it was cool, it could also get pretty embarrassing at home. "I think you'd be good at it."

Janelle smiled. "Thanks," she said.

"So what are you guys doing this weekend?" said Mori. Gloria shrugged. She didn't want to say "nothing," that would sound....about as boring as it was.

"I don't have any plans yet," Scuba said.

"Me neither," said Emilia.

"Well, I was thinking we could have a club party or something," said Mori. "My mom is offering to host it."

"Sounds like a great idea," Scuba said.

"Well, I guess I'll go, even if Scuba is there," said Emilia with a sly smirk.

"I foresee that it'll be a great party," said Janelle. The group paused and looked at her.

"Really?" said Mori.

"No, I was just making a joke," said Janelle, ducking her head. Gloria laughed, putting a hand over her mouth.

Mori grinned. "Well, I'll let you guys know what time to come over, I'm thinking about lunchtime on Saturday."

"Sounds great," Gloria said with a nod. What did they do at parties? It had to be more exciting when everyone had superpowers. Then Gloria got a sinking feeling. What if they all had cool stuff they did with their powers? She had to figure something out before Saturday.

"I can bring some pizza, my parents can pick something up for us," said Emilia.

Without warning, the whole group was drenched in cold water. Mori looked up just in time to see a solidified shadow, which had carried the water above them dissipate, and they heard Derek cackling just a few tables over, along with some of his no-power friends.

Gloria inhaled some of the water in surprise, then coughed it out and shivered slightly. Scuba shook his head to get the water off, sending bubbles flying from his hair. He shot Derek a glare across the room. A cloud of steam rose up from Emilia.

"Hey Emilia, nice sauna you've got going on there!" Derek called, which of course only made her blaze hotter and create even more steam.

"You alright?" said Mori to Gloria. One of his doubles was already running off to get towels from the gym.

"Oh, yeah, I'm fine," Gloria said. "Just...you know, cold and wet."

"Looks like Derek is going to get detention," said Emilia, looking on as a teacher dragged Derek out of the cafeteria by his arm. "That doesn't fix the fact that our food is soaked, though."

"Seriously," Scuba said. "And you can't blow-dry your lunch, trust me, I've tried. It doesn't work."

"Um, you didn't try to use your powers to blow dry food, did you?" said Emilia. "You blow bubbles."

"Hm, that may have been part of the problem..." Scuba admitted.

"I'll get us some new lunch," said Mori, sending off several duplicates. His first returned with the towels and the group moved to another table to dry off better.

"Doesn't he have anything better to do? Like, eat his own lunch?" Scuba muttered.

"Apparently not," Mori said.

This was the third real prank of the year, at least that Gloria knew about. A few weeks ago, Derek had put glue on the backpacks of the club members, making them stick to their backs. Emilia's had stuck to her hair. Before that, he had slicked the floor outside the club room during a meeting.

"I'd say he's jealous of not being in the club, but he could have joined anytime he wanted," said Emilia. "I mean, so long as he stopped telling everyone he was going to grow up to be a villain and stopped pranking us."

"I told him that two weeks ago," said Janelle with a sigh. "He just laughed and said he was just fine with the way things are."

"Figures," Gloria sighed. "Sounds like he's got his mind pretty made up. At least there's just one of him, though."

"Well, there were two at the beginning of the year," said Mori. "Some girl named Tami who could phase through walls. Her family moved, though, so it's just him and his little fan club over there now."

"I wouldn't mind him so much if he only picked on us," said Janelle. "But he bullies a lot of the other students, too. He takes his whole 'villain' aspirations way too seriously."

"I hear that's more common these days," said Mori. "Especially with kids whose parents don't have powers or never became heroes. Lack of structure or something, I guess."

"Derek's parents don't have powers," said Janelle. "His mom works as an actuary."

"Makes sense," Scuba said. "Though it's a huge bummer for those of us that have to deal with Derek now."

"Yeah," said Emilia with a sigh. "I've imagined setting his pants on fire a lot. Or his backpack, or his desk… But then we'd just get in trouble."

"Yeah…." Gloria said, frowning. Something about this didn't feel quite right to her, and it wasn't just her damp socks.

"It's pretty lame, though," said Mori. "I mean, we're supposed to be heroes, and yet we just have to sit back and let the bad guys get away with stuff just because we're not adults yet or whatever." He sighed. "I can't wait until we're older and we're allowed to actually do something about this sort of stuff."

"No kidding," Scuba agreed. Gloria nodded.

The bell rang, startling the group.

"See you guys after school," said Janelle, and she took off, as did Mori and the others.

CHAPTER THREE

After her last class of the day, Gloria headed straight for the club meeting. She ducked around elbows and backpacks as she wove through the hall. On the way, she heard a commotion ahead and stopped suddenly at the sight of Derek just around the corner. He was using his powers to hold a smaller boy upside down while the boy kicked and yelled, his face bright red from all the blood rushing into his head.

"Let me down, I'm gonna puke!" the boy yelled. The other students stood back nervously, leaving a wide circle around Derek and the boy.

"Ha, your face looks like it's going to explode," said Derek with a cackle. Gloria scowled and felt her face flush. Before her sense of reason could stop her, she marched up to Derek.

"Hey, cut that out," she said. "Let him down."

Derek smirked as he turned to face her. "Why, do you want to hang around instead?" His three-dimensional shadows rose up behind him menacingly. She felt herself starting to lose her nerve, but she couldn't back down now.

"Just let him down," she said. She crossed her arms and planted her feet firmly. "It's not funny."

"Weird, I mean, I'm laughing," said Derek. "Here, you give it a shot and see what you think." The tendrils of darkness darted forward and wrapped around her middle.

"Hey!" Gloria said sharply. She threw out her hands in front of her, sending a sudden blast of air and sand directly at Derek's stomach. "Get off me!"

The sand shoved Derek ten feet down the hall, taking his feet off the ground and severing his tie to the shadows and forcing him to release both Gloria and the upside-down boy. The boy caught himself with his hands and tumbled to the side, looking relatively unharmed.

Derek gave a cough as he stumbled to his feet again. The blast had knocked the wind out of him, and he seemed quite surprised at how far he was from where he'd been standing.

The students standing around cheered, and the boy Derek had tormented gave Gloria a grateful smile as he picked himself up.

"You okay?" Gloria asked, glancing over at the boy.

"Yeah, thanks," he said. Down the hall, Derek narrowed his eyes at Gloria, then ran off, away from the scene.

"Well...great, um, see you," Gloria said, then headed off towards the club meeting. She was glad Derek had left, and, now that she could think about it, it felt good to make him back off. Mori was right, sitting back while he picked on people sucked.

Almost the entire club was there already. Only Emilia came in after her, her eyes wide with excitement and her hair- were the ends of it catching fire? Hopefully not.

"I heard what you did," she said. She raised her hand for a high-five. "Totally awesome."

Gloria smiled and returned the high five. "Thanks."

"Wait, what happened?" Scuba asked, looking over from his seat at one of the desks.

"Gloria kicked Derek's butt," said Emilia. "She sandblasted him when he was picking on Greg."

"Woohoo!" Scuba cheered, and he threw his hands in the air and released a cascade of bubbles into the air.

"Kind of," Gloria said with a shrug. "Well, okay, I did sandblast him...."

"And he ran off like a chicken," said Emilia. "Everyone is talking about it, you're totally the school hero now."

"Really?" Gloria asked. It had only happened a few minutes ago. How had everyone already heard? "I mean, you're making it sound way cooler than it was."

"Come on, you're the first person to stand up to Derek like that," said Emilia. "And everyone else is saying you're a hero, so that pretty much settles it for me."

"Well... I did think it was kind of overdue for someone to make him back off," Gloria agreed. "I mean, he'll only get worse if we just let him."

"True, I mean, I know we're supposed to leave it to the teachers, really, but..." said Mori. "I think it's great that you stood up to him. It's a pretty brave thing to do."

"Thanks," Gloria said with a smile.

"He won't stop picking on people," said Janelle. "I mean, he might not go after Gloria again, but he's definitely going to try to keep doing what he's been doing."

"Well, maybe it's time to stop waiting for the grown ups to fix it," said Mori. "Maybe it's time we all started taking action ourselves. This is a club for future heroes, after all. Why not be heroes now?"

"We do have a zero tolerance policy for bullies at school," said Emilia cocking her head back. "I don't see any problem with reminding him of that."

"It's better than just ignoring him," Gloria said. "That didn't seem to be working at all. Even if the teachers punished him, it didn't stop him."

"Exactly," said Emilia with a nod.

"Well, in the meantime," said Janelle, "who is bringing what for the party this weekend?"

"You know what I'll bring?" said Scuba with a mischievous grin.

Emilia shot him a look. "I swear if you say bubbles-"

"Bubbles!" he exclaimed, and once again he released a cloud of bubbles into the air around him.

"Well, you can write that down, if you must," said Mori. He pulled a notebook out of his backpack. "I made a sign-up list."

Emilia snickered and Mori passed the list around. "You're such a nerd, Mori," she said.

"A... SUPER nerd," said Scuba enthusiastically.

"Don't make me come over there," Emilia warned.

Talk shifted away from Gloria's stand-off with Derek and toward plans for the party. Even though the moment had passed, however, Gloria still felt a warmth inside from the discussion. She was a hero.

CHAPTER FOUR

"Come in, come in!" Mori's mom gushed to the kids on her doorstep. Gloria and Emilia had arrived at about the same time that Saturday, both bearing snacks they'd brought from home. "Just put all of that on the counter over there," they were directed, and then they joined Mori and Scuba in the living room. Scuba had already set hundreds of bubbles floating about the house, and one popped on Emilia's face as she entered. They'd barely found a couch to sit on before the doorbell rang and Mori's mom ran off to bring in more guests.

Mori's living room had a TV and gaming system all set up and ready to use. Extra chairs had been pulled out from the kitchen, and there were board games on the coffee table.

"Cool," Gloria said, looking around. She chose a spot on one of the couches, then tried to push herself up into a comfortable sitting position. "What games do you have?"

"Well there's Dance-Dance Revolution, Mario Kart, Wii Bowling, and Halo," said Mori. "Those are all of the multi-player ones, anyway."

"I vote Halo," said Emilia. "I rock at that game."

"Really?" said Mark, another one of their club friends. "Not Dance Revolution? I mean, you're a-"

"I'm a what, Mark?" said Emilia sharply, giving him a hard look. Mark stopped himself.

"-a…. really good dancer," said Mark nervously.

Emilia gave him a narrow-eyed, suspicious look. "Well, I like Halo. I'll totally kick your butt in it, too."

"Just don't melt your controller," Scuba teased. "Or make anything catch fire, deal?"

"Oh please, I haven't melted a controller since I was six," said Emilia, and she stuck her tongue out at him.

Janelle frowned. "You didn't have superpowers yet when you were six…"

"Who's hungry?" said Mrs. Sang. She brought in a tray set up with the snacks the kids had brought, plus some homemade cookies and lemonade. Gloria laughed and Scuba gave Emilia a suspicious look while snacks were passed around.

"I'll just be in the other room if you kids need anything," said Mrs. Sang cheerfully, once everyone had taken their fill of snacks. "Don't have too much fun!" She laughed, then left.

"Is it just me…." Gloria said between bites of a cookie, "or do moms get kinda weird when friends are around?"

"It's definitely not just you," said Mori with a sigh. "Honestly, I've been in this club for over a year, and she still thinks I need her help making friends. She's been almost more excited for this party than me."

"I mean, it's not bad," Gloria said with a shrug. "But it is weird."

"Yeah, you might even say our parents are… SUPER weird," Scuba said, barely able to keep from laughing at his own joke.

Emilia rolled her eyes and picked up a controller. "You're super weird," she muttered. "Pick up a controller and stop pretending to be funny."

"I am *hilarious*," Scuba protested. He scooted closer to the tv and grabbed a controller.

Mark and Janelle picked up the other two controllers, and Mori made a waiting list for people who wanted a turn on the gaming system. Everyone without a controller either settled down to talk and watch or play one of the board games. Mori and Gloria sat down with another girl, Amanda, to play a game of Chinese Checkers while they waited.

"So where's your dad at?" said Amanda to Mori. She moved the pieces on the board with her telekinetic powers.

"He's at work," said Mori, "running a drug bust or something with the police." He gave a wry smile. "Hero parents, am I right? They've always got unpredictable schedules."

"At least there's always a cool story," Gloria said. "They never have a boring day."

"True," said Mori. "It'll be cool when we're doing things like that. My mom likes to remind me how lucky I am to get to be a hero and have powers. You know, since so many kids dream about it but not everyone makes it." He grimaced. "She especially likes to bring it up when I have a test."

"My mom had me take applied combat classes when I was little," said Amanda. "My brother never got his powers, she was so disappointed."

"Ouch, that would be rough," Gloria said. "I was kind of starting to worry about getting powers. I'm glad it didn't end up like that."

"No kidding," said Mori. "I think my parents would disown me if that happened."

Mrs. Sang ducked her head around the corner. "Mori, I just got a call from your dad; he needs some backup. I should be back within an hour or two. Are you kids alright here by yourselves for a bit?"

"Yeah mom, no problem," said Mori. "I'll call you if we need anything."

"Good, good, I'll see you soon," she said, then took off down the hall. Mori shook his head.

"There you have it, unpredictable schedules," he said. "I'm glad she stopped calling a sitter every time that happened, I only managed to convince her I was old enough to babysit myself just last year when I got my powers."

"Dang," Gloria said, shaking her head. "Though...with your power, I guess it makes sense. You can babysit yourself."

Mori grinned. "Yeah, it was a pretty compelling argument."

"Haha, got you, Janelle!" Emilia crowed from the gaming station. Janelle's character fell to a blast from behind. "I'm coming for you next, Mark."

A moment later, the room and the tv screen suddenly went dark, making Janelle jump with surprise.

"Ugh, power outage," Mori groaned. "I'll go get some flashlights"

When he made it to the door, Austin, who was sitting by the window, gave a terrified squeal and leaped away from the window, where the shadows had moved suddenly and unnaturally toward him. Gloria scowled. Emilia narrowed her eyes.

"Derek," she spat. She stood up. "I'll go chase him off." Gloria and Emilia dashed out of the room.

Scuba hesitated, then stood and followed them. "I'll come with you," he called.

They headed out the back door, toward the garage. It was pitch black, impossible to see their own feet in front of them. Then Emilia ignited fire all over her body, becoming a human torch. The shadows shrank back from the fire.

"Can you see him?" she asked Scuba.

Scuba shook his head, squinting at the edges of the light to try and catch a glimpse of Derek. Something moved over by the garage door. Emilia blasted fire right in front of the figure, making him stumble back sharply in surprise. The shadows around them retreated several inches.

"Quick, get him!" Emilia exclaimed, her palms smoldering.

Scuba thrust out his hands, sending a blast of bubbles at Derek's face. Gloria sent a wave of wind and sand crashing in on him, causing him to stumble back into the garage door.

"You are not invited," Gloria said.

"Thank goodness for that," said Derek with a snicker. "Then I'd be at the wrong house." The shadows lashed out at them, and the bubbles stopped as Scuba tripped over them. Emilia put out her fire and caught Scuba before he could hit the ground. Derek escaped Gloria's wind and took off running and laughing.

"Come and catch me, heroes!" he called back to them. Scuba scowled after him.

"He's such an idiot," he muttered.

"Yeah, let's get him," said Emilia, and she took off running after Derek, igniting her flames again. Gloria was right behind her, the air swirled around her and it was as if her feet barely touched the ground as she ran. Scuba hesitated again, then ran after them.

Outside on the lawn, Derek was booking toward the street. Emilia shot fireballs at him, which he deflected with his shadows and laughed, making her angrier. Scuba caught up to Emilia and grabbed her arm.

"Hey, let him run," he said. "I think he gets the message."

Gloria paused and bit her lip as she glanced back at Scuba.

"Yeah," she said finally. "Scuba's right. He won't be back today."

Emilia stopped and scowled, glaring at Derek as he disappeared down the street.

"Alright," she said. "Let's go back inside."

They went back to the party, where everyone was quiet, sitting in the dark and some using their phones as lights. Everyone looked at least a little nervous, though Janelle looked particularly upset.

"It was Derek alright," said Emilia. "He's gone now, though. We chased him off."

Mori frowned.

Janelle sat quietly in the corner, eyes downcast and arms about her knees. She looked the most nervous out of everyone.

"How did he know when my mom was going to be gone?" he said after a moment. "I mean, if he'd pulled this stunt while she was here, he'd be in big trouble."

"Maybe he was just waiting until she left," Scuba said.

"It'd still be a lucky break that she left at all," Gloria pointed out.

"Yeah, he could have been waiting out there all day for nothing, " said Mori. "And it's weird that he even knew about the party, too."

Janelle's eyes welled with tears as she whispered something.

"What was that?" said Emilia. "What'd you say?"

"I… I said I told him," said Janelle, her voice shaking.

"About Mori's mom leaving? Or just the party?" Scuba asked.

"Both," she said. "He… he said he wanted to join the club, and that he wanted to apologize for what happened at school. It didn't seem like a good time to bring it up before, so I invited him to the party. He said he was worried your mom would be mad if he just showed up uninvited, so I suggested he come by with snacks after she left…"

Scuba sighed, shaking his head.

"Well, looks like that isn't quite what he had in mind," he said.

"No kidding," Gloria agreed.

"How did you not know he was going to do this?" said Emilia, scowling. "You're a psychic, you're supposed to be able to see the future."

Janelle sniffled and wiped at her eyes.

"I don't see everything," she said. "Some things I can see and some things I can't, I don't know why, I just…. I thought he really wanted to join the club."

Amanda glared at her. "Well that's just great," she snapped. "Anything else you've told him about? Any future parties you've invited him to before we even plan it?"

"I didn't- no, I wasn't," Janelle stuttered. "I'm sorry, I just… I should go." She picked up her bag from beside the armchair near the tv.

"No Janelle, it's alright," said Scuba quickly. "It's not your fault, I mean, you were just trying to be nice."

"Yes, let's invite all the supervillains to Mori's house," said Amanda sarcastically. "That'll be real nice, right?"

Amanda was unable to speak further as she was engulfed by a massive wave of foamy soap bubbles.

Emilia burst into laughter. "Oh man, oh man Amanda, you look a little washed out."

Emilia and Scuba were shoved backward by a telekinetic blast. The bubbles were parted by Amanda's telekinesis as she stepped out, glaring.

"Not funny," she snapped.

Emilia glared at her and looked about burst into flame when Mori split into several copies of himself, sending two by Amanda and two by Emilia.

"That's enough," he said firmly. "Scuba, clean up your bubbles. Emilia, don't set my house on fire. Amanda, I think Janelle understands that inviting Derek was a bad idea, no need to push the subject." He looked over at Janelle. "If you really want to leave, you can, but we'd really like you to stay, Janelle."

Janelle nodded meekly and sat down. Gloria sat next to her to comfort her as Mori's doubles disappeared, and Scuba walked through the bubbles, soaking them back into his skin like a sponge as he went.

The party settled down again after that. Mori found the breaker box and got the lights back on, and Derek didn't return. Mrs. Sang returned a while later with pizza, and nobody spoke a word of the incident.

CHAPTER FIVE

As the term grew closer to the end, the weather cleared up from it's chilly, cloudy gloom. With it being brighter and warmer out, just about everything seemed to be looking up. At least, that's what Gloria thought as she headed to school.

School was a lot less nerve-wracking with the rest of the super club as her friends; she didn't know how she had managed before.

The students were standing up to Derek more and more, and Derek himself had been escalating his antics in response. Students in the club had things stolen from their backpacks and lockers, and shadows jumped at them from dark corners to scare them. Emilia was always quick on the scene, chasing him off or fighting him for the stolen objects, and one or more of Mori's doubles were usually on hand, just in case.

Then, one day, they came into the club classroom, and the smell of paint stung their nostrils as they opened the door. The tables and chairs were overturned and scattered, and the whole room was splattered in red.

Mori froze in the doorway and scowled, wrinkling his nose.

"Oh great," Gloria said with a scowl. "Everything in here is going to be ruined, it'll take at least a few days to clean it off."

"And that's assuming it all comes off," said Mori, shoulders slumping. "This is ridiculous, this isn't even just our club meeting place, it's a classroom, too. There's no way he can get away with something like this."

"Well, we can report it," Scuba said. "But what are we supposed to do? He'll keep doing stuff like this as long as he goes to the school."

"That doesn't mean we have to make it easy for him," Gloria said, crossing her arms.

Emilia came up behind them and growled. "Ohhh he's going to pay for this."

"Right?" Gloria said. "Man, if I were the one making decisions about the school, he'd be cleaning this up himself."

"What do we do?" said Mori. "Maybe I could call my parents, they're home more often now that they've got a new member on their team."

"We should go find him," said Emilia. "We're the heroes in this school, it's our job to make sure stuff like this doesn't happen."

"He's probably still around here somewhere, too," Gloria agreed with a nod. "Let's go find him."

Gloria led the group back through the halls. Everyone split into groups in search of Derek. A few minutes into the search, Mori stopped her.

"One of my doubles found him," he said. "He's just outside the school."

"Great," Gloria said. They ran out to meet up with the others. None of them had a real plan, but they weren't just going to let Derek get away with it either.

When they got out onto the lawn out to the side of the school building, Derek was standing almost as if he were waiting for them. His face split into a wide grin.

"Not fine art enthusiasts, then?" said Derek.

"Fine art?" Gloria scoffed. "I don't think you have that kind of talent."

"Ah, well, everyone's a critic," said Derek with a shrug.

"You're going to get back in there and clean it up," Emilia snapped.

"Or what?" said Derek with a laugh. "You'll tell on me?"

"You think that's all we could do?" Gloria said, stepping closer.

"Yeah," said Derek, crossing his arms as his shadows gathered behind him. "I think that's pretty much it."

Gloria scowled and blasted him back with a powerful gust of wind. Derek grimaced against the wind as he was thrown back, though he caught himself with his shadows and sent them flying out to pin down the others. Emilia shot fire at the shadows, searing some of them so they disappeared with a hiss and allowing the others to advance. They were all engaged in fighting Derek's shadows, on their way to get at Derek himself, when suddenly they were all trapped in violet energy bubbles, forcing Derek's shadows to disappear. The principal came walking forward the group, flanked by Mori's parents and members of their hero team, and Janelle.

"I think that's quite enough," said the principal. To a woman wearing violet he said, "Thank you, Deirdre, you can let them go now." The bubbles disappeared, and the students were left standing around shamefacedly on the lawn. "My office. Now."

They followed her back into the building, exchanging glances.

One by one, they were sent into the office and berated by the Principal for engaging in such "dangerous and reckless" activity and were told that all of the students would be assisting in cleaning the club classroom. If anything happened like this again, they would all face suspension for a week, at the very least.

They cleaned the club classroom in angry silence, shooting Derek glares if he got too close. After that, Derek seemed to be keeping his head down to avoid suspension. The tension between Derek and the hero club grew like the stench of sweaty socks, going longer and longer unwashed. While no one was hurt or in any particular danger, the school lawn suffered bald patches where Emilia often walked. In the class that Emilia shared with Derek, a decorative fern wilted under the wrathful heat that emanated from her.

It was just the second day after the incident that Mori came to lunch with a sour, pained expression that he tried to hide behind his folded arms.

"What's wrong?" Gloria asked after a few moments of awkward silence.

"Nothing," Mori mumbled. "Just tired."

"Is it the paint thing?" said Emilia. "We're all mad about that, we don't mind if you want to talk about it."

"No, it's not-, it's just my parents," said Mori miserably. "My mom is in the hospital. There was... an incident with work."

"What happened?" Gloria asked with a frown. "Is she okay?"

"It's the team technopath," said Mori. "turns out he's a dirty traitor, working for some foreign agency or something. They found out he was leaking secrets and there was a confrontation. My mom was hurt pretty bad, they say she'll pull through but she might... she might lose her legs." Mori's face disappeared back into his arms on the tabletop.

The group exchanged anxious glances a moment, then Gloria put a hand on Mori's arm.

"I'm sorry," she said. "That's awful."

Mori didn't say anything, too embarrassed to lift his face and show the tears burning in his eyes.

"When do you see your mom next?" said Emilia. "We could go to the hospital with you, bring some flowers and cards."

Mori sniffled and nodded. "If you want, yeah," he said. "I'm going to see her this afternoon."

"We'll come, then," Gloria said. "I'm glad she'll pull through, at least."

"Thanks," said Mori. "I think she'll appreciate that."

"Did they catch the technopath, at least?" Scuba asked.

"Yeah, though a lot of other people on the team were hurt, too," said Mori. "It was all a mess."

"Dang," Scuba said, shaking his head. "That's messed up."

"Yeah," said Mori with a sigh.

The group fell into an uncomfortable silence as they all thought of their own parents, and what dangers they could be facing at that moment.

Of course, things didn't get much better after that. After a few weeks went by, Derek started working mischief again, as the entire club could have predicted. By the end of the year, he'd done enough property damage to the school to get expelled. Mori's mom came home from the hospital with a wheelchair, which took some adjusting for the whole family. Even so, with Derek gone, and Mori's mother on the mend, things started to settle back to normal.

The next year passed as the best year for the hero club, with mounted respect from the rest of the student body, and not too infrequent parties and activities hosted by the club members' parents. Golden as the year felt, the end of it came with the sad understanding that they'd be splitting up. Janelle was going to a private school, the rest of the students were either moving or attending different high schools. Gloria, Mori, Emilia, and Scuba, however, all were met with the same great news. They had all been accepted to a school dedicated to young aspiring heroes, all with superpowers. The club would be splitting up, but they, at least, would be staying together.

CHAPTER SIX

The first day of high school, the foursome quickly found each other in the cafeteria and claimed a table.

"So, how are classes going for you guys?" Emilia asked.

"Pretty good, for me," Gloria said. "They don't seem too hard, at least not yet."

"Yeah, too bad Janelle isn't around to help anymore, though," said Emilia. She heated her burrito with her hand, then nearly flash-fried it when she was startled by a loud laugh and a crackle of lightning nearby. The group glanced over at a far table by the cafeteria door, where a boy in a high-collared cloak had created sparks of lightning above him while laughing at a joke. The boy who had told the joke shifted farther away, like he regretted his choice of where to sit.

"Almost forgot about him for a minute," said Mori with a sigh. "That's Carter, he's in one of my classes. It figures that a school like this would have at least one aspiring super-villain in it."

"Huh, not even subtle," Gloria said, looking over at Carter. "Kinda reminds me of Derek, you know?"

"They're always the same," said Emilia, shaking her head. "Overly dramatic, gothic clothing style, creepy smiles…"

"Not to mention the mushroom cloud he made in my chemistry class," said Mori. "Nearly scared a few doubles out of me." Gloria laughed, then tapped the table next to her food thoughtfully.

"Ever wonder if fate has something to do with it? I mean, like, with powers," Gloria said. "There is an interesting trend among supervillains, after all."

26

Mori shrugged. "Well, I wouldn't say fate, but I know some statistics that definitely reveal a pattern. A lot of the factors that give these things away are noticeable pretty early on."

"Hm, yes, statistics," said Emilia with a solemn nod. Then she coughed into her hand. "Nerd."

"Yeah, I mean, it's like foreshadowing, except in life," Gloria said, ignoring Emilia. "It'll probably be even more obvious in hindsight if you think about it."

While she was talking, another girl approached. She had curly blond hair and green eyes. Gloria didn't recognize her, but Emilia seemed to.

"Hey, what are you guys talking about?" she asked, sliding in next to Emilia.

"Oh, hey, Alexandria," said Emilia. "We were just talking about the guy over there, totally going to be a supervillain, am I right?" Emilia pointed to Carter. His cape billowed behind him from a gust created by the cafeteria door, revealing a couple of gadgets on his belt.

Alexandria snorted in laughter before taking a bite of her sandwich. "Carter? Nah, trust me, there's no way."

Mori glanced at Alexandria. Gloria raised her eyebrows.

"He's in my science class," Mori said, "he nearly blew up the lab. It made a mushroom cloud, like those scary cartoon ones."

Alexandria rolled her eyes. Gloria guessed she didn't have much experience with supervillains.

"Probably an accident, he's no good at chemistry," Alexandria said. "But being bad at science isn't exactly evil."

Overy by the cafeteria door, Carter laughed loudly again, and the lights in the ceiling above him flickered and buzzed in an ominous fashion. A thin bolt of electricity leaped down from the lights and shocked one of the boys at the table out of his seats, making Carter laugh even harder. Emilia gave Alexandria a pointed look, her hand extended toward the scene.

"Yeah, how do you explain that?" Scuba asked. He had grown taller over the last summer, making him disproportionately gangly. He looked like he was about to fall off the edge of the bench he was sitting on.

"Okay..." Alexandria said, a bit hesitantly. "I mean, he's a clutz and a technopath. His powers are pretty closely tied to his emotions. Especially his laughter emotion. So, you know, probably an accident...?"

Emilia rolled her eyes. "Laughter isn't an emotion, Alexandria. I mean, fireballs don't blow up behind me when I laugh. My powers don't do anything when I laugh, only when I'm angry or upset."

"So his powers are more fun," Alexandria said flippantly. She took another bite of her sandwich. "Seriously, you'll want a different candidate for villain speculating. Once you get to know him, you'll realize it's ridiculous."

"Unless he's manipulating you," Mori muttered into his milk carton. The others fell silent, remembering Mori's parents and their technopathic traitor. Before it had happened, that would have seemed ridiculous too, and yet...

"Excuse me?" Alexandria asked, raising her eyebrows and leaning forward. The table fell still. This girl looked ready to fight, Gloria thought, bracing herself.

"Well," Mori looked over at her, "I mean, it's a thing that psychopaths do; they act likable and nice to manipulate people." He shook his head. "And anyway, technopaths are statistically more likely to be supervillains, and when you combine that with how he dresses..." He glanced over at Carter. "Well, it's kind of weird that they let him into the school in the first place when you really think about it."

"Okay, seriously, this started kind of funny, but now it's just getting rude," Alexandria said. "Talk about being judgemental." She shook her head, looking at them with disbelief and irritation.

"I'm not being judgemental," said Mori irritably. "I'm just saying that he falls into a certain profile. It's not my fault that you're so intent on ignoring it."

"Falling into a profile does not disqualify you from going to school," Alexandria said, crossing her arms defiantly. "Especially when you haven't done anything wrong. And he's not a psychopath, either."

"I dunno," Gloria said, glancing at the others. "I think Mori has a point. I mean... he just zapped a guy."

They could see Carter was already being abandoned by the people he had sat next to.

Alexandria stood. Her lunch tray was in her hands. She gripped it so fiercely Gloria worried she would hit one of them over the head with it.

"It was probably an accident," she said irritably, "and I'm not hungry anymore." Then she left, dumping her mostly uneaten lunch in the garbage as she stalked off. Carter left close behind her.

"Interesting," Gloria said.

Mori watched them go glumly. "You don't think I was being judgemental, do you?" he asked. Carter's cape swooshed behind him, disappearing around the corner of the cafeteria door like the flicker of a shadow.

"Of course not," Gloria said. "We all saw the guy, definitely creepy. She's just in denial."

"Well, it's not anything we can't handle," said Emilia. "We've handled school villains before, and that was back when we were in a school for normal kids. This is a school for heroes."

"Yeah, shouldn't be too much of a problem," Gloria said. "And he'll know he's outnumbered, maybe that'll encourage him to lay low during school."

"We can hope so," said Mori. "Who knows why he even came to a school like this in the first place." His expression darkened. "Maybe to get an in with the competition."

"Yeah," Gloria agreed, her brow furrowing. That thought made her stomach turn.

"Maybe he won't be as bad as Derek," Scuba suggested hopefully.

"Or maybe he'll be worse," said Mori. Scuba shrugged, turning his attention to his sandwich as he filled it with chips.

"Well, it doesn't hurt to keep an eye on him, at least," said Emilia. "I mean, under the circumstances, it would be irresponsible not to." She cast a glance to Gloria for confirmation. She was, after all, their unofficial hero expert.

"Yeah, we should definitely keep an eye on him," Gloria said with a nod.

Soon, the bell rang to mark the end of lunch. The rest of the day passed in a blur of introductions, get to know you games, and disclosure documents. As mundane as the first day was, it still held promise. They could already tell the classes would involve superpower application. Now superpowers were the norm, instead of the elite.

That afternoon, they met up at Mori's house for some lemonade and snacks. Mori helped his mom put it all together and they all settled on the couches to talk about their classes and eat. Mori sat by Gloria once everyone was settled, his plate loaded with crackers and peanut butter.

"There's a guy in my class, this dude Elliot," said Emilia. "He's basically invincible, except for his peanut allergy."

"So he could take out a tank, but my cracker here would kill him?" said Mori. "That's messed up. They'd have to keep that deep under wraps when he works."

"No kidding," Gloria said, shaking her head. "That would be so annoying; what if you had to save someone who was eating peanut butter or something?"

"Maybe he'll get a special peanut resistant suit," Scuba said.

"Can you imagine making super suits as a job?" said Mori. "You'd get the weirdest stuff. Like this girl in my class grows extra arms. How do you account for that?"

"I have no idea," Gloria said. "That kind of job would have to have pretty intense science involved."

"So are we going to meet up and stuff all the time like before?" said Emilia. "Or are we just going to count the school as our new club?"

"Well, if we have a club now, it'll have to be more specific," Scuba said. "Or, we could," he shrugged, "not worry about a club and just hang out."

"I like just hanging out," said Mori. "I mean, I figure we're already planning to be a hero team together later, right? I think just being a group of friends is enough." He glanced at Gloria. "What do you think?"

"Yeah, I don't think it needs to be an official club anymore," Gloria agreed. "I mean, we're pretty officially all friends, that works."

"We could always get coordinating tattoos!" Mori called unnecessarily loudly.

"Haha, Mori, very funny," his mom called back from the kitchen. Gloria laughed.

"A fun idea, but no," Gloria said. "I mean, imagine, if we ended up with different teams or something, could get a bit awkward."

Mori looked a little concerned by the idea of them being on different teams, though he didn't say anything. Instead, he looked down at his lemonade glass. Emilia noticed this and snickered.

"Nah, I think we're pretty much stuck together as a group," she said. "Which, you know, is great for Scuba, but kind of a bummer for me."

"Oh, get over yourself," Scuba said, throwing a chip at Emilia. Emilia swatted it away and tossed a chip back at him. Mori tossed a chip at Gloria, hitting her just below the eye. The chip fell and stuck in her hair, and Gloria cast him a sideways, slightly confused glance, before looking down to pick it out.

"Oh, sorry, I-uh, was aiming for Scuba," Mori stuttered. Emilia cackled as his face flushed bright red.

"Um, okay," Gloria said. She disentangled the chip successfully and put it on a napkin. "So, first impressions wise, what'd you guys think of the student body? Aspiring villains aside, I think it looks pretty exciting."

"I think it looks great," said Emilia. "A few potential new friends, nobody as cool as you and Mori, of course, but I think I'll like it here anyway."

"I wonder if, like, English and stuff'll be easier here," Scuba asked hopefully. "I mean, since we've pretty much decided on our careers as superheroes, some of that stuff won't be as relevant, right?"

"No such luck, Scuba," said Mori's mom, rolling in on her chair to gather the dishes. "You still have to fill out police reports, paperwork and documentation, write articles to support law enforcement changes, and all sorts of technical writing."

"Yeah, but Shakespeare isn't gonna help with that, is he?" Scuba asked. "At least technical stuff makes sense."

"Maybe to you," said Emilia. "Shakespeare is just stories and reading and stuff. I'd take an easy Shakespeare class over some paperwork class any day. And don't bash the Bard."

"A guy can dream," Scuba said wistfully, then licked off the crumbs from his plate.

"Well when we get one of those crazy villains who uses old literature trivia questions as their bomb diffusing passwords, you'll be glad someone was paying attention in English," said Emilia, crossing her arms.

CHAPTER SEVEN

Gloria and Scuba had History with Carter after lunch the next day, and, Gloria had to admit, there could definitely be something to Mori's suggestion that Carter was manipulative. With a few exaggerated smiles and a pun, Scuba crumbled under Carter's pressure.

"So, Scuba had a bit of a lapse in judgment earlier," Gloria told the group after school. "He agreed we'd all meet up with that Carter kid and his friend after school."

"I was nervous, I couldn't think of a good reason to say no," Scuba said defensively.

"How about the creepy way he asked?" Gloria said.

"What was I supposed to say? I can't because that was too creepy?" Scuba asked. Gloria rolled her eyes. Emilia snickered.

"Anyway, so we're meeting up in the far field," Gloria said, turning to Mori and Emilia. "If you guys wanna come."

"Well, we can't just leave you two to suffer alone," said Mori.

"Even if it is Scuba's fault," said Emilia elbowing Scuba in the ribs as she walked past.

"Alright, let's go," Gloria said, taking the lead. Scuba sighed defeatedly behind her, shoving his hands into his pockets and falling into step.

"Maybe Scuba could trip down the hill and be our excuse to bail?" Emilia suggested, following with Mori.

"Gee, thanks," Scuba said sarcastically.

"I'm sure it'll be fine," Gloria lied. "I mean, we don't have to do anything too crazy, you know?"

"Yeah," said Mori. "And, you know, might as well get to know his powers while he's scoping out ours."

"Exactly," Gloria said with a nod. She was definitely glad the whole group was going together, she didn't know what she would have done if it was just her and Scuba with Alexandria and Carter.

Emilia suddenly frowned, sniffing. "Scuba... do you smell like... mangos?"

"Why yes I do," said Scuba proudly. "It's a new scent of soap I bought."

Emilia sighed. "You bought it? Yourself?"

"I always like to buy new soaps to try out," said Suba. "And I always smell clean, and fresh," he extended an arm for Emilia to smell. She swatted his arm.

"You smell like a fruit basket," she said.

"Well at least I don't smell like a campfire," said Scuba. "You literally smell like a fire hazard."

"I am a fire hazard," said Emilia with a gleam in her eye. "Want to see?"

Mori shushed them. They had reached the field by this time and looking back at the school, Gloria could see Carter and Alexandria coming out one of the back doors.

The group fell silent as they watched the two approach. Carter lugged a wagon full of electronic materials and parts behind him. Alexandria appeared somewhat nervous, though Carter met their looks with a steady gaze, unphased by any of the tension hanging in the air.

"Hey," Gloria said as they approached, breaking the silence.

"Hey," said Carter. "I see you brought the rest of your friends. That should make things more interesting."

"Yeah," Gloria said. Her stomach seized suddenly with nerves. What did he mean by 'more interesting?'

"Well," said Carter, clapping his hands together. "Why don't we see how well we can travel together?" He glanced about the group. "I figure a good number of us can fly, but Mori... will probably need some help."

"Alright. Well, I can probably help Mori out," Gloria said quickly.

Mori smiled a bit at that. "Thanks," he said with a nod.

"Great, so that's Mori taken care of," said Carter. He waved his hand, sending tendrils of electricity flying from his fingertips to snatch up the materials he'd brought in his wagon. The gears and wires and metal parts all floated up, swirling about him in the air a moment before assembling as his mind directed, creating a metal platform with some sort of engine beneath it. Alexandria watched it all with wide, fascinated eyes as the platform settled at Carter's feet, and Carter let his hand drop.

"I can take people on this," Carter said, gesturing to the platform. He glanced again at Gloria, and Gloria remembered he didn't know her power yet. Then he glanced at Emilia, probably the only other one in the group whose power he hadn't learned one way or another.

"Well, I can already fly," said Emilia, crossing her arms under his gaze. "So that just leaves Alexandria, really."

"I'll ride with Carter," Alexandria said without hesitation. "I definitely can't fly."

"That's everyone, then," said Emilia. She rolled her shoulders, aching to get this done and over with.

Carter stepped onto his platform with Alexandria, and the machine crackled with his electricity as parts shifted to lock about their feet to hold them into position. Then the engine hummed and the platform hovered upward a few inches.

"Let's do one lap around the field," said Carter. "Try to keep close and figure out some kind of formation, yeah?"

"Yeah, sounds cool," Scuba said with a nervous shrug. He'd never actually tried flying before, Gloria remembered, but at this point, it was either that or fly with Carter.

"Let's go," Gloria said, she reached out with her hand and pulled the air around her, lifting her and Mori into the air. Emilia burst into flame and took off like a human rocket, followed by Glori and Mori, and finally, Carter and Alexandria in the back on his hovercraft. Scuba made a giant bubble surround him and, to his great relief, he was able to maneuver it into the air with a surprising amount of agility. He nearly rammed into Gloria as he tried to catch up, but she deflected him gently with her desert wind.

Carter kept something of a distance, watching the rest of the group ahead of him with a look of intense, studious concentration.

Suddenly, his hovercraft shuddered, and with a spark of electricity, a screw came flying out like a bullet straight at Scuba, popping his bubble. Scuba cried out and plummeted toward the ground. Emilia dove to try and get to the ground first, but Scuba managed to recreate another bubble and bounced lightly off the grass.

Everyone landed, with Carter and Alexandria landing last. Alexandria was struggling to withhold a laugh, and Carter seemed almost… frustrated.

"Well," said Carter, pausing to take a deep breath, "I think that went well. I mean, obviously, my hovercraft could use some work." Alexandria snorted and Carter gave her a sharp look. "But other than that, I think we kept together pretty well."

"Yeah," Gloria said, glancing over his hovercraft. Carter seemed disappointed in how his platform had worked, but it seemed more like he was disappointed that Scuba hadn't hit the ground. "I think we got a pretty good....evaluation of things."

"So next," said Carter, clapping his hands together again, "let's figure out costumes. I mean, obviously, I have something in mind already for myself," he gestured at his flowing black and dark blue cape with the pointed collar. Scuba jumped slightly at the sudden motion, now standing in shock behind Emilia.

"Ah yes, well," said Mori, "I don't think we really need to decide all of that right now."

Carter shook his head. "Gloria will be blowing a lot of dust into the air," he said. "We should wear something to protect our eyes; that'll also help if Gloria has to put up some sort of dust smokescreen, and of course there's nothing worse than getting soap in your eyes." He grinned at Scuba, who almost didn't dare breathe under his gaze.

"Yeah, the last thing we need is to get blinded in the middle of something," Alexandria said.

"Alright," Gloria said with a shrug, frantically trying to deflect Carter's intimidation and end this exercise as quickly as possible. "So we incorporate eye protection into our costumes."

"I could make some," Carter suggested, "if you-"

Mori cut him off. "Actually, I think we should all make our own," he said, exchanging another glance with Gloria. "Otherwise it might not fit right, you know?"

"Oh, alright," said Carter, scowling somewhat at the suggestion. "Makes sense, I guess."

"I think that covers everything," said Emilia, glancing at the others for confirmation.

"Yeah, I think so," Gloria agreed quickly.

"And I have homework to get to," Scuba sputtered out, almost shouting the words in his panic.

"Okay," said Carter. "Well, maybe we can do some more practice like this another time."

"Maybe," Gloria said flatly. They all left quickly before another word could be said.

The group separated, and Mori and Gloria started off walking home together.

"So," said Mori, "that happened."

"Yes, yes it did," Gloria said. "Scuba almost died."

"Yeah," said Mori. "I mean, I was worried about him scoping out our powers, not homicide. But at least he's not making costume pieces for us; imagine what he could do with that."

"No kidding," Gloria said with a shudder.

"Well, hopefully, it won't escalate from this point," said Mori. "If we just avoid him for a while, maybe he'll give up and settle for laying low until graduation or something."

"Hopefully," Gloria said, though she didn't believe that in the slightest. "If not....well, we're definitely not letting him near Scuba again, at least. Imagine if he'd been alone with them?"

"No kidding," said Mori. "I don't think any of us should be alone with them. I mean, I don't know who was worse, Carter trying to manipulate his way to murder, or Alexandria getting a kick out of the whole thing like it was some big joke."

"Me either," Gloria said. "Carter definitely scares me the most, though. At least Alexandria is open with what she's thinking. On the bright side, if we keep an eye on her, we might get clues as to what Carter gets up to."

Mori nodded thoughtfully. "Good idea," he said. "I'll see if I know anyone who she talks to."

"Do you....even know what her power is?" Gloria asked, frowning at the thought. "I don't think she said....only that she can't fly."

"No, I don't know," said Mori, frowning. "That's a problem. They learn everything about us, but we know nothing about them."

"Not the best situation to be in," Gloria agreed. "I mean, is she keeping it a secret or something?"

"I guess," said Mori. "Though I don't think we'll be able to figure out why until either we find out her power or they do something with it, you know?"

"Yeah," Gloria said. "Keeping it secret is definitely....weird. Not a great sign."

Mori sighed. "Man, for some reason, I never thought being a superhero would be this complicated when I was a kid."

Gloria laughed, bumping his shoulder. "Everything seems easier before you try doing it."

Mori bumped her back. "Well, maybe not for you."

"And what's that supposed to mean?" Gloria asked, cocking an eyebrow.

"I dunno, you make it look easy," said Mori. "You always seem to know what to do with stuff like this. If I were the leader, I'd definitely mess all this up."

"Well, I'll definitely let you keep thinking I know what I'm doing," Gloria said with a shrug. She smiled and glanced over at him.. "But I don't think I'd call myself the leader, I mean, we're not even a club or anything anymore."

"Still, you're pretty much the leader of the group," said Mori. "I know I'd follow you anywhere."

"Oh...thanks," Gloria said, turning her head momentarily and tucking her hair behind her ear. "I guess I'm glad I haven't led anyone off a cliff yet or something like that."

"Eh, even if you did," said Mori, grinning a bit, "you have wind powers, remember?" He stopped; they'd come to his house. "Well, I'll see you tomorrow, yeah?"

Gloria smiled.

"Yeah, see you tomorrow." She turned and headed on towards her own house before it could get awkward; there was a faint wriggling sensation in her stomach threatening to make her say something stupid if she lingered too long. Now that would be embarrassing.

CHAPTER EIGHT

The group met in the halls before class a few days later, as they always did. Now, however, Mori was glancing over his shoulder.

"No sign of Carter, thank goodness," he said. He sat against the wall beside Gloria, then propped up his feet on his backpack. "It's not just me, right? He's been practically stalking us ever since the whole 'practice team-up' thing."

"It's not just you," Gloria confirmed. She shook her head. "It's like he's there every time you turn around, right?"

"He keeps asking if I want to practice with him and Alexandria again," said Emilia. "Doesn't even mention you guys, just me. Maybe he's gonna try and kill me next."

"You haven't agreed to meet with him, right," Gloria asked. Emilia could handle herself in most situations, but she didn't trust her alone with Carter.

"I'm not an idiot," said Emilia. "I just keep saying I'm busy."

"Maybe you could tell him you just don't want to?" Scuba suggested hesitantly. Gloria shot him a sideways glance.

"You're the one that encouraged him in the first place," she reminded him. Scuba rolled his eyes.

"I said I was sorry. Doesn't almost dying mean I've suffered enough?"

"Well we'll forgive you when he leaves me alone," Emilia muttered. "Otherwise, I'm getting a restraining order. Can teenagers get that? Is that a thing?"

"I don't think so," said Mori. "Especially what with us sharing classes with him. We'll just have to... wait it out, I guess, try not to aggravate him into action in the meantime."

Gloria nudged Mori and nodded towards Alexandria, who had just appeared around the corner and was heading towards them. She flashed them a smile that seemed much too deliberate.

"Hey, guys, what's up?" Alexandria asked.

"Not much," said Mori with a shrug, trying not to look uncomfortable. The others nodded. Scuba didn't dare try to speak this time.

"Okay, well..." Alexandria scanned the group, "Carter and I haven't seen much of you the past couple days, we just wondered if something was going on?"

"No, nothing's going on," said Emilia, a bit quickly. "Just busy with school, you know?"

"Alright. It just seems like you've been avoiding us a bit," Alexandria said, cutting right to her point. "Carter specifically."

"I almost died!" Scuba exclaimed. Emilia smacked his arm.

Alexandria rolled her eyes. "It was an accident, obviously, and you're fine," she said. "Honestly, no one got hurt."

"This time," Mori said quietly.

"Excuse me?" Alexandria asked, an eyebrow raised critically. Gloria suddenly didn't like that she was sitting and Alexandria wasn't, it made her feel like a mouse about to be pounced on by a cat.

"No offense," said Emilia, coming to her rescue. "You're just, you know, a bit overprotective of Carter."

"He's my friend," Alexandria shot back, turning her gaze on Emilia. "So, yeah, obviously I'm not going to like it if people assume he's some kind of psychopath."

"Even if he is one?" said Mori.

Alexandria scowled, clenching her fists. "It was an accident, and avoiding him won't make him any less accident-prone."

The group fell silent a moment as the implications of that hit them. She was right, after all, hiding out from him wasn't going to stop him, especially when they had classes together.

"Look, if you don't want to hear it, that's your decision," said Emilia. "We're not stopping you from hanging out with him. We're just going to... keep our distance for a bit."

"You guys are idiots," Alexandria said, rolling her eyes. She turned on her heel and stalked off, quickly disappearing down the hall.

The group exchanged nervous glances as she left.

"Well, she's definitely going to be a supervillain sidekick," said Emilia under her breath.

"Oh yeah," Scuba agreed with a nod.

"Maybe we should be more careful," said Mori, pulling his backpack closer to him. "I mean, if we make him angry, he might... you know, cause another accident."

"It's a bit late for that," Gloria said, chewing her lip thoughtfully. "I mean, we definitely got on Alexandria's bad side now, and she'll definitely tell him."

"Well, so long as we're not meeting with him alone, he can't do much," said Emilia. "I mean, he's in a school full of superheroes. That's a lot of witnesses, and a lot of people who can intervene with their own powers."

"That's a good point," Scuba said. "I mean, we'd have been a lot safer if the whole school had been at the field with us. And he can't hit us all with screws... can he?"

"Speaking of which," said Emilia, frowning. "What can Alexandria do? I mean, she's practically Carter's sidekick already, and we know nothing about her powers except that she can't fly."

"I don't know...," Gloria said with a frown. She had forgotten they didn't know Alexandria's power. "We should probably find out."

"Well we can't ask her," said Emilia. "I mean, not after today."

"I know someone who has English with her," said Mori. He'd been working this out since he'd spoken with Gloria about it a few days before. "I'll talk to him, see if he can ask her during class or something."

"Great," Gloria said. "Just let us know when you find out."

Mori nodded. The bell rang, and they dispersed.

CHAPTER NINE

Mori and Gloria shared History class just before lunch. It was a normally uneventful class, though Mori seemed a bit nervous during it. Then, suddenly there was a flash of green light by Mori, and a piece of paper fluttered in the air before he grabbed it.

"It's from my friend, Ed," said Mori. He unfolded the note and scanned it quickly. "He's the one with a class with Alexandria. Apparently, her power is energy manipulation."

"Hm, interesting," Gloria said. "Could be worse, I guess."

"Yeah," said Mori. "I mean, not too dangerous, not like shadow manipulation or anything."

"True," Gloria said. "Though, honestly, Alexandria seems plenty dangerous on her own, even if she didn't have powers."

"Yeah, well, hopefully, she won't do anything crazy," said Mori. "So long as we keep our heads down like we've been doing, we shouldn't have any incidents."

"Right," Gloria said with a nod. The teacher cleared his throat suddenly.

"Mori, Gloria, is there something you two would like to share with the class?"

"Uh, no, sorry," Gloria said, her face flushing.

They fell silent for the rest of class, then went straight to the cafeteria when the bell rang. Everyone assembled quickly with their lunches at the usual table, though Emilia looked like she was bursting with news.

"Guys, did you hear?" she said, her hand tapping on the table. "Alexandria attacked a guy last period."

"What?" Gloria said, blinking in surprise. "Attacked someone? What happened?"

"Well, some guy in her class was talking to her, just kind of normal conversation stuff, then she just stands up and decks him," said Emilia. "Knocks him clean off his chair. She's got detention now, but it was savage."

Mori grimaced. "It wasn't Ed, was it?" He shook his head. "I shouldn't have made him ask her about her powers. I guess she figured out that he was friends with me or something."

"Dang, well, so much for not provoking them," said Emilia. She took a drink from her milk carton. She nearly coughed on it when she saw Carter approaching, his cape billowing ominously behind him.

"Seat's taken," Mori blurted nervously, instinctually, as Carter stopped in front of the table.

"Yeah, I know," said Carter curtly. "I'm looking for Alexandria. Have you seen her?"

"Not since this morning," Gloria said. "And sounds like I should count myself lucky for it."

Carter scowled deeply. "And what's that supposed to mean?" he asked darkly.

"She decked a guy in English today," Mori said. "Just...blew up at him."

"What?" said Carter. "Why? What'd he do?"

"They were talking," Gloria said with a shrug, trying to play it casual. "But it's not that hard to get her worked up about whatever, is it?"

"Not without good reason," said Carter coldly. "I don't know what your problem is with her; she never did anything to you."

Gloria glanced over at him, then back at her food. Don't act intimidated, she thought.

"Well if you don't know, just think it over," Gloria said. "It'll come to you."

"Actually, I don't think it will," Carter said testily.

"Well, for starters," Gloria said, glancing at the others, "it's not Alexandria that's the real problem."

Scuba glanced at Carter nervously and quickly turned back to his sandwich. Carter scowled.

"Oh, right, I'd almost forgotten," he said. "You all think I'm some sort of supervillain, right?" He clenched his fist. "All I've ever done is try to be your friend."

"Which, you know, wasn't that hard to see through," said Mori under his breath.

42

"Well, if you're all so convinced," said Carter, glaring at them, "then there's no point in me trying to be nice, now is there?" Carter's scowl deepened, and electricity sparked about his fingers. Then, suddenly, he turned and stormed away, his cape whipping behind him. A metallic, electric taste lingered in the air even after he was gone, and the group sat in stunned silence before Mori spoke.

"Well... I think he's provoked," said Mori quietly. Gloria nodded, letting out her breath.

"I think that's safe to say, yeah...."

"What do we do about it?" said Emilia, looking somewhat nervous. It was her, after all, that Carter had seemed to be targeting next.

"I guess... we just keep our eyes out, like we've been doing," said Mori. "If he's got anything planned, it'll definitely happen soon now. We just have to figure out what it is before it happens."

"How are we supposed to figure that out?" Scuba asked. "We don't have a psychic anymore, you know."

"Well... maybe we could call her?" said Mori. "Does anyone still have her number?"

"I think I do," Gloria said. "We could try that, yeah."

"When do you think you can get ahold of her?" said Mori.

"I'll try calling her tonight," Gloria said.

"Great," said Mori. "You can tell us what she says tomorrow." Gloria nodded.

"Alright," she said with a sigh.

That evening, Gloria found Janelle's number and made the call. It took several rings before Janelle's mom picked up and gave the phone to Janelle.

"Hey Gloria," she said. "What's up?"

"Eh, school and stuff," Gloria said, lying on her bed. "We've got another Derek over here. How's your school?"

"Pretty good," said Janelle. "I mean, it's no hero school like yours, but it has a good chess club and volunteer program."

"That's cool," Gloria said. "So....I kinda have a question for you. Um, a favor."

"I'm gonna guess you want me to make a prediction for you?" said Janelle. "You know my visions aren't a hundred percent, right? I mean, unless it's something fixed like test answers, I can't guarantee everything will happen the way I foresee it will. So if this is about you and Mori..."

43

"What? No!" Gloria said, sitting up. She could hear Janelle laughing on the other end. "That's not-well it's not that. No, it's about this future villain kid. He's kind of worrying us, we're hoping....you might be able to give us a heads up on if he's got something planned?"

"Well, if he's a future villain, he probably does have something planned," said Janelle. "But if you're looking for something that'll happen soon, I can take a look. Got anything specific, like tomorrow or the day after? A specific moment I can check on?"

"Moment? Not really...." Gloria said, hesitating. "Maybe like, if it's gonna be this week?"

"Okay, but vague questions get vague answers, just a warning," said Janelle. The other end went silent for a moment. "I see... a lot of conflict at the school, fighting. Not words fighting, like combat with powers and electricity everywhere. Someone crying in the hallway, a black eye, someone else is seriously injured, a scream, flashes of pink energy... wow, you're in for a rough week from what I can see. Oh, and you'll fail all your classes." Another pause. "Well, that's a week's summary for you. Maybe you should stay home sick for a while?"

Gloria groaned, flopping back onto the bed.

"That's sounding really tempting," she muttered into the phone. "Well, thanks, at least now we can brace ourselves."

"Do you want me to call someone?" said Janelle. "I mean, I guess you can't call the police for something that hasn't happened yet..."

"Yeah, we'll have to take it as it comes," Gloria sighed. "We'll report it when we get there."

"Well, be careful," said Janelle. "Let me know if I can help, okay?"

"I will," Gloria said. "And thanks again."

"No problem," said Janelle. "And remember, not everything is set in stone. The vision was blurry as it is, so... maybe there's still a chance to stop it? Good luck."

"I'll keep that in mind," Gloria said. "At least you don't have supervillain stuff at your school, right?" she added.

Janelle gave a snort. "No, no villains here," she said. "Just a few somewhat obnoxious athletes, though even then our circles don't really cross much. Let me know if you manage to avert the end of the world at your school."

Gloria laughed. "Definitely. Well, I should get to my homework. Maybe I can at least prevent the part where you foresee me failing all my classes. I'll talk to you later."

"Yeah, talk to you later."

CHAPTER TEN

The next day, Gloria was summoned to her counselor during her first-period class to discuss her suddenly failing grade. All her classes were marked with a failing grade. Gloria felt her heart trying to escape her ribcage, that wasn't possible!

Sure enough, it was soon discovered to be a computer error, and Gloria was sent on her way.

Out of Janelle's predictions, Gloria wasn't expecting this one to be first. While she was relieved it would be corrected, the fact that it was Carter's doing, undoubtedly, was not a good sign.

At lunch that day, everyone else in the group seemed irritable, and Emilia melted her lunch tray before making it to the table. Mori sent a double to help her carry her second tray.

"Let me guess," Gloria said, setting her tray down by Mori. "You guys failed your classes, too?"

"Yes," Emilia snarled.

"Twenty guesses why," Mori muttered. Then he sighed and ran a hand through his hair. "Didn't take him long, did it? I doubt this'll be the last thing he does, either. How did the talk with Janelle go?"

"Well, no good news," Gloria said. "She said I'd be failing my classes, so that happened. That's kind of....the least of it, though."

"The least of it?" said Emilia nervously. "What else is he planning? Is he planning to kill someone? Me?"

"Are my parents really going to send me to boot camp?" said Scuba. "That's what they said they'd do when they saw my grades."

"Yeah, well," Gloria said hesitantly. "See, I asked Janelle to take a look at this week, for an idea, you know.....aside from grades, there was a lot

46

of fighting, serious injury, crying in the hallway or something, and a lot of electricity and pink energy. Three guesses who those come from."

The table went quiet, each of them somewhat frightened by the prospect of what Gloria was suggesting.

"That's... not good," said Mori. "It sounds like he's planning some sort of big attack on the school, or at least on the students." He glanced briefly at Emilia. "Man... and this week? We don't have much time."

"Well... we have to stop him," said Emilia determinedly. "I mean, we call ourselves heroes, but we haven't done anything yet, not here. Maybe it's time we stepped up, like with Derek. I mean, if the whole school is in danger... did Janelle say there was any way to stop it?"

"She said it was fuzzy, not set in stone," Gloria said. "But we'll have to move fast, I mean...."

"There's only one way to stop him, then," said Emilia. "No time to waste waiting and watching and hoping he doesn't come out of nowhere with something like he did with this."

"We have to tell the teachers," said Mori.

"Mori, that literally never works," said Emilia.

"And we don't have any proof," said Gloria. "I mean, he'll just say they were accidents, like Alexandria does."

"Punching Ed in the face wasn't an accident," Scuba said.

"Yes, but she got detention, not Carter," said Emilia. "If we want to stop him, we need to get evidence."

"Well, maybe someone can talk to Alexandria, see if she knows anything?" said Mori. "Not one of us, obviously, she hates us. I'll ask Ed if he has any ideas. He's the one who shares a class with her, anyway."

"Great," said Gloria. "Talk to Ed, and we can regroup behind the PE building after school and discuss whatever you guys find out."

"In the meantime, don't be alone on your way to class," said Emilia.

The others nodded solemnly in agreement, then jumped, startled by the sound of the bell.

Emilia was the first out of class, and she started out for the PE building. On her way through the empty gym, she startled at the sight of Carter storming her way.

"There you are!" he snarled, his fingers crackling with electricity that jumped to the floor around him.

"Ahh!" Emilia cried out, and she put up a wall of fire between them. The ventilation shafts above them ripped from the ceiling and slammed down over the flames, smothering most of them. The others came in just as Carter stepped over the rubble.

"Emilia!" Scuba cried out, and Carter was suddenly blown back with bubbles. Mori split into five doubles, several leaping onto Carter through the bubbles to try and pin him down. Carter fought hard, clawing at the arms of the doubles and his fingers crackling and sparking, popping the bubbles and shocking two doubles. The group saw Mori wince with pain as his doubles bled from where Carter's nails raked their arms.

Emilia ran forward to stop him, her fist blazing with fire as she tried to punch him. Mori's doubles disappeared and Carter blocked the attack with his forearms, glaring fiercely at her. He threw his arms out and moved to the side, sending Emilia sprawling. He turned to face the others, the hem of his cape dusting over the fallen Emilia as he turned.

Gloria raised her hands, sending a sandblast to try and knock Carter off his feet. He coughed and covered his eyes, but stood his ground. Emilia leaped up and cuffed him on the side of the head with another flaming fist and a kick to the leg that sent him staggering before his knees hit the ground. Still, he wasn't done. His hands exploded with electricity, blasting out at the group and causing them to quake with pain.

Gloria gritted her teeth, then reached out and pulled the air into a cyclone around Carter, distracting him, and Scuba tackled him from behind to stop the electricity blast. They both fell, and Carter elbowed Scuba in the side, blasting him with the worst of the electricity while he pulled his cape up to shield against the wind and sand that still blew. Mori's doubles rushed to help Scuba.

Everything fell into a blur of motion, sand, and electricity. Everyone was squinting against the wind and sand while lashing out, sometimes accidentally hitting one another instead of Carter. Emilia was in the thick of it, her fire blazing up her arms as she fought furiously, further infuriated by the stinging pain of electricity.

Then, there was a sickening snap, and Carter screamed. Everyone backed off immediately, and the dust settled. Carter lay on the ground holding his leg in one arm and the side of his face and the other arm hung limp and curled by his chest, his eyes streaming from pain, soap, and sand. They could see the area around his ear was burned badly from where Emilia had hit him, and serious bruises were welling up everywhere else. Finally, something in his right leg had snapped and was bleeding heavily.

"Guys," Scuba was the first to speak. "Uh, we need to call someone."

"Call an ambulance," Mori cried out. He split, sending a double to find a teacher. "We need to call an ambulance!"

Scuba nodded, fumbling with his phone as he pulled it out. Unfortunately, there was no cell service in the school.

Gloria crossed her arms and looked away from Carter, her stomach turning over. Emilia's fire extinguished, and she stood to the side wringing her hands. Part of her wanted to help Carter, but the other part was terrified by the sight of what their powers had done, and afraid of making it worse. Thankfully, it wasn't long before sirens wailed at the front of the school, and Carter was wheeled away on a stretcher. All of this took place before Alexandria even got out of detention.

CHAPTER ELEVEN

There was silence at the dinner table in Gloria's house that night. Her parents were disappointed, that much she could tell, but beyond that... they hadn't discussed what had happened. The tension was building, however, and it was only a matter of time before they cracked.

Gloria kept her eyes on her food as she shifted it around her plate, not daring to be the one to break the silence.

Her mom finished eating first and spoke the moment she'd put her fork down on her plate.

"Gloria," she said, her voice tight. "I believe you owe us some explanation."

Gloria slumped back in her chair.

"I'm sorry," she mumbled. "We didn't mean for anything like that to happen....."

"You're sorry?" her mother said darkly. "You 'didn't mean' to attack another student after school? He's in the hospital now, Gloria. Of course, your father and I have graciously offered to help pay for the expenses, which means we will not be going out of state for vacation this summer."

Gloria shrank further into the back of her chair. There wasn't anything she could say that wouldn't make it worse, so instead, she put a bite of food in her mouth.

"We talked to the school as well," said her father. "You'll be suspended for the week, and have two months of detention. We are very disappointed in you, Gloria. I thought we'd raised you better than this."

"I know," Gloria said miserably. "I'm sorry."

"For now... go to your room after you finish eating," said her mother. "You're grounded until your detention ends in two months, perhaps longer." She stood. "Your father will keep an eye on you tonight. I have to go to work." She stormed out, and Gloria could see her chair had at some point in the conversation become crusted with ice. Gloria grimaced, then pushed her plate away.

"Um….I'm going to bed, then," she said as she got up. "Gnight."

Her father didn't respond, his eyes on his plate. Gloria sighed and went up to her room. She flopped down on the bed and stared at the ceiling. This was not how things were supposed to happen.

The week was a lonely one, each member of the group grounded and isolated from the others. At least when they were allowed in school again, they had detention together. They were supposed to be silent, but… they found ways to pass notes. Mori sat next to Gloria every time, and Emilia brought donut holes that they ate when the overseeing teacher wasn't looking.

Even so, the two months couldn't be over fast enough for Gloria. It was only a few weeks, however, before Carter returned.

If it could be argued that he didn't look the part of a villain before, he certainly did now. His expression was constantly a dark scowl, accentuated by the angry red burn scar that engulfed his left ear and part of his face. He walked with a pronounced limp, his previously broken leg now bound up in some sort of mechanical brace that squeaked when he walked. People scattered when he came down the halls.

After they had been released from detention that afternoon, the group gathered to talk, though carefully marking the time, as they were still grounded.

"He's still wearing that cape, too," said Emilia, as they discussed Carter's reappearance. "He's even got a villain name now, Dr. Vile."

"I definitely get the feeling things are only going to get worse from here," Gloria said. Scuba shook his head.

"This is bad."

"Yeah," said Mori quietly. "I mean, he attacked Emilia, but I don't think he'll figure that justifies what happened."

"I guess so, yeah," Gloria said, her arms crossed. "Hopefully he doesn't come after us for revenge or something, though."

"He probably will," said Emilia quietly. "I saw Ed in the halls today, he said Alexandria was acting aggressive during class again."

Gloria sighed. "Oh, great."

"Yeah, that could cause some problems," Scuba agreed. "But...I gotta get home right now…."

"Right, me too," said Emilia. "See you guys in detention tomorrow…"

"Yeah, see you," Gloria said. The group dispersed uneasily home.

A few days later, Mori split on his way home from detention, sending a few doubles to find Alexandria. Ed had managed to contact him by teleporting a message, saying Alexandria had let slip during class that she and Dr. Vile had another plan. He intended to find out what that plan was.

Alexandria had a good deal of space left between her and other students as she walked, and Mori couldn't blame the others based on the poisonous looks they got if they came too close.

"I hear you're planning something," said Mori, one of his doubles coming up alongside Alexandria. Alexandria glanced at him out of the corner of her eye.

"Oh yes," she said with sinister sarcasm, "quite extensive plans. They involve homework, mostly, and quality time with quality people. That does not include you, by the way."

She didn't slow, if anything she quickened her pace.

"I'm guessing you mean Dr. Vile, then," said Mori, emphasizing the name Carter was going by now. "What, only back a few weeks later and he's already planning his next strike? You'd think he would take the time to recuperate in between schemes."

"Interesting you should say so," Alexandria shot back. "You seem to have recovered rather quickly from the fact that you and your friends scarred him for life for absolutely no reason. We're not scheming."

"Like you weren't scheming before?" said Mori. "When you weren't scheming to mess up everyone's grades? Come on, even you can't call that an accident."

"Oh, so you still think what you did was fair?" Alexandria asked, her expression darkening. "That's pretty pathetic, Mori, considering that 'scheme' was a prank with no lasting effects. You need to get yourself a better hobby."

"We stopped him before things got worse," said Mori firmly. "That's what heroes do. They stop the bad guys."

"I've got news for you," Alexandria said, turning to face him. This emphasized the fact that she was about an inch taller than Mori, and took full advantage of it. "You aren't heroes. You're just thugs."

Her hands crackled with veins of pink energy, barely contained.

Mori paled slightly but held firm. "And what, you think you're the hero?" said Mori. "If you don't know what you've turned into, then honestly, you're the only one who hasn't caught on yet. He's manipulating you, Alexandria."

Alexandria's eyes flashed angrily, her irises turning the same pink as the energy in her palms for a brief moment.

"If you guys are the heroes," she said angrily, "then I don't want to be on your side."

She turned as if to leave, then suddenly spun back to face him. He barely registered the pink encasing her fist before she sent him sprawling backward. "So leave me alone!"

The energy blast was hot and painful, and so intense that the double she'd hit disappeared before he even finished falling. The real him, walking home, stumbled from the sensation, and the other doubles glared at her as terror gripped their collective guts.

"Villain," they said, before they disappeared as well, out of harm's way. Mori, the real Mori, sat down on the sidewalk a moment to catch his breath, shaking from the encounter. Well, he didn't find out what they were planning, but it was clear that Alexandria had no qualms now in attacking whoever questioned her about it. But there wasn't much he could do, not with him and the others trapped by detention and still grounded. He took a deep breath, then stood, and continued home. His mom was expecting him.

CHAPTER TWELVE

The group was finally free from detention as the Christmas season came around, and at the very least Dr. Vile seemed to be keeping to himself in the meantime. Mori had been using his doubles to keep an eye on him every now and again, and he'd caught several large packages being delivered to Carter's house. He didn't dare get closer yet, however, as he didn't want to risk getting detention, or worse, get expelled. Like Carter, Mori had to bide his time in the meanwhile, and so the Christmas season was left in peace by an unsteady stalemate.

Now that they were out of detention, at least, Mori hoped he and the group could meet up after school. In the morning, before classes started, he went to find Gloria, then froze when he saw her standing by her locker. It was covered in tinsel, lights, and gold and silver orbs. A cluster of mistletoe trimmed into the shape of a heart hung from the top, and her expression was one of pure joy. A twinge of jealous anger flared in Mori's stomach. Who…?

Then he noticed everyone looking at him, down to the other girls giggling near Gloria's locker. Gloria was looking at him, too.

"Uh… hi," said Mori, blushing deeply. "I-uh was hoping to talk to you…." Gloria smiled shyly.

"Yeah?"

Mori's mind went blank. What was he planning to talk about, again? "Uh… um, well, uh," he stuttered. "Uh, nice locker, right? It- uh, decorated. Yeah. Merry Christmas."

Gloria laughed and nearly tackled him in a hug.

"You're the best, Mori," she said. A locker door slammed nearby, and Mori saw Alexandria disappear around the corner.

Mori smiled, hugging her back and feeling somewhat dizzy. He considered telling her he wasn't the one who did this, he really did. But… no one else seemed to be taking any credit for it, and he probably wouldn't get the words out anyway, so he did what he figured was the only logical thing in this situation. He kissed her.

Gloria leaned into him and kissed him back, and everyone in the hallway cheered.

When they broke apart, Mori finally managed to get out a legitimate sentence. "So, uh, want to hang out after school?"

Gloria smiled.

"Sure," she said. "Got something in mind?"

"Um…" ah, right, a date. Not as a group. "It's a surprise."

"Well, I can't wait," Gloria said. The bell rang and Gloria pulled away, shouldering her bag. "See you after school."

"Yeah," said Mori with a smile. "See you." Once she was out of sight, Mori sent a double to class while he ran back outside. He needed to plan an impromptu date, fast.

By the time school was over, Mori had, he hoped, set up a date that both fit the unexpected surprise in Gloria's locker, and was even better. A candlelight early dinner set up at his place, with three well-decorated Christmas trees surrounding the table and paper snowflakes hanging from the ceiling. After Gloria's last class, three doubles were waiting for her with a well-cushioned wooden armchair.

"Ready to go?" said the first copy, gesturing for her to take a seat. Gloria hesitated.

"Uh…yes?" she said. "Where….?"

"My house," said the copy. "I, uh, couldn't find a carriage in budget, so I figured a Mori-powered ride could work… If you want."

"I mean, we could just walk," Gloria said. "Your house isn't that far."

"Yeah, okay," said Mori sheepishly. The other two copies disappeared with slightly disappointed expressions. Mori blushed. "So, uh, you ready?"

Gloria smiled and took his hand.

"Let's go."

Mori led the way to his house, which his parents had kindly agreed to vacate for the afternoon, though they told him they'd be back by eight. Mori pulled out Gloria's chair for her, abandoning the whole doubles thing for now. The dinner, cooked by his dad, was sirloin beef, vegetables with gravy, and sparkling apple juice. After the somewhat rocky start, everything went well, or at least Gloria seemed to be enjoying it.

"So, got any big plans for Christmas?" said Mori.

"Mm, not really," Gloria said. "Just the usual family stuff. What about you?"

"Well, my family was planning on going to Florida for a week," said Mori. "But we'll be back by the week of Christmas. Maybe we and the others can do a Christmas white elephant thing or something?"

"Yeah, that would be fun," Gloria said. "I don't think Emilia will be out of town, at least."

"Scuba mentioned to me he would be here that week," said Mori. "And it'll be nice to do something together for the holidays."

"Away from all the school drama," Gloria agreed. "I'm definitely excited for a break from that."

"No kidding," said Mori. "Alexandria attacked one of my doubles a few weeks back, though they haven't done anything major lately as far as I can tell."

Gloria winced sympathetically.

"Yeah, at least there's that," Gloria said. "Alexandria's definitely a time bomb, though."

"And her explosions are usually followed by some big scheme from Carter," said Mori. "Though he seems to be taking a break for the holidays, at least. I guess even supervillains gotta enjoy the holidays."

"Lucky for us," Gloria said with a smile.

"Yeah," said Mori, smiling back. He lifted his glass of sparkling apple juice for a toast. "Merry Christmas."

"Merry Christmas," Gloria said, tapping her glass against his.

CHAPTER THIRTEEN

After the break, Emilia came running to the group before classes, two blank papers in her hands.

"Guys, look what I saw Carter throw in the trash," she said.

"Blank paper?" Gloria asked. "What about it?"

"No, not blank," said Emilia. She heated her hand beneath the paper. "Look." Numbers appeared on the paper, faintly brown, written in what apparently was invisible ink. "It's some sort of code. Maybe Alexandria gave them to him, or she was going to come get them later."

"Yeah, maybe," Gloria said, moving closer to take a look.

"Any idea what it means?" Scuba asked, poking his head over their shoulders.

"No idea," said Mori. "But we should get to work decrypting them. Let's see if we can find a codebook or something in the library during lunch."

"Definitely," Gloria said.

"Man, he's stepping up his game," Scuba said, shaking his head. "It's in a code, and invisible."

"It must be important to put that much work into it," said Emilia. "I mean, it's almost like voluntary math."

"Seriously," Scuba said. "Oh great....now we basically have to do extra math!"

"Well, my mom always did say hero work comes with paperwork," said Mori. The bell rang to go to class. "Well, I'll see you guys in the library later."

"Yeah, see you," Scuba said, not as enthusiastically.

The group spent the next month working on the code, and Emilia kept bringing more papers that she caught Carter dropping into bins or tucking behind books in the library. Every day, after eating lunch and after school, they were in the library, surrounded by papers, notebooks, and volumes on different kinds of codes. Mori even pulled out a book on computer codes, just in case that led anywhere, but no luck.

Valentine's day came, and when the bell rang for them to go to lunch, all the lights in the school went out with a quiet "pop."

There was a cry of surprise, and quite a deal of scuffling before flashlights on phones began lighting up Gloria's classroom. The power didn't seem to be coming back on, so the students quickly left to try and find lunch.

Gloria noticed some pink lights down the hall as she made her way to the cafeteria. Mori went to join her but was pulled aside by Carter into a side hall. Mori yelped.

"Okay, here's the deal," Carter hissed. "This is a surprise for Alexandria. You won't interfere, no one will get hurt, and you'll keep your group out of our way during lunch."

"And what if I don't?" Mori snapped.

Carter's eyes narrowed. "Then I'll tell Gloria who really decorated her locker," he said. "Or did you forget about that? I'm sure she'd love to know that you lied."

Mori's eyes widened. "You-"

"Yeah, me," said Carter, "and no, I don't have a crush on her. I do, however, need you and your friends to stay out of my way. Just for today, just for my little surprise lunch with Alexandria. Got it?"

Mori hesitated, but he had to admit, Carter had him. If Gloria found out he'd lied… Mori nodded.

"Fine," he said. "But just for lunch today, and you better not do anything to hurt anyone."

Carter grinned, then took off to the cafeteria, running as fast as his leg brace would let him. Mori sighed, then hurried to catch up to Gloria. Emilia had already joined her.

"Hey guys," he said. "Where're you headed?"

"Cafeteria, I guess," Gloria said. "Hopefully they'll still have lunch."

"Yeah," said Mori. "Hey, so uh, I heard that Carter was going to be busy doing some lame romantic thing in the cafeteria today, so maybe we could take advantage of him being busy and hit the library some more?"

"Oh," Gloria said. "Yeah, I guess we could."

"Ugh, lame," said Emilia. "I'll go find Scuba and tell him, I guess." She headed off, lighting her way by flaming hands until a teacher barked at her to put it out.

Mori hesitated. Now was probably the best time, Emila would be back soon. He stopped and reached into his backpack. "Uh... Gloria?" he said. "I, uh, made you something."

Gloria turned, smiling.

"Oh? What is it?"

It wasn't very impressive, not compared to whatever Carter probably had planned for Alexandria. But... it was better than nothing. He pulled out a handmade valentine's day card, cut in a heart shape from red cardstock and decorated with a superhero crest in the center. Inside the crest, it read "you're my super Valentine!" He handed it to her with a small bag of chocolate truffles. "Uh, happy Valentine's day," he said.

"Aw, it's great," Gloria said with a smile. She took his hand and kissed him on the cheek. "Happy Valentine's day."

Mori smiled. At least she seemed to like it. Still, he couldn't forget the decorated locker and the awful realization that he'd been manipulated. All that time he'd spent focusing on dating Gloria during the holidays, losing track of Carter's movements... It all made sense now.

Emilia came back around the corner with Scuba.

"Well, let's go to the library," Emilia said glumly.

"Yeah, let's go," Gloria said with a smile, pulling Mori along with her by his hand.

Lunch went by slowly, painfully, and they were back again after school. Before Gloria and Mori showed up, however, Emilia caught up to Scuba.

"Hey," she said. "I got something for you."

"Huh?" Scuba said, turning to face her. "Um, what is it?"

"Here," said Emilia, handing him a folded card. He took it and opened it. The moment the card was opened, it ignited itself in a brilliant burst of flames. Scuba yelped, dropping the card, then sneezed.

He blinked in surprise for a moment, then laughed. Emilia laughed as well, loud and hard, though quickly stamped out the fire with her foot. Mori and Gloria arrived together while they were still laughing.

"What's so funny?" Mori asked.

"Arson," Scuba said.

"I...worry about you two," Gloria said.

They laughed again, and Mori shook his head in bemusement.

"Come on, let's get to work," he said.

On the way to the library, Scuba tapped Emilia on the shoulder.

"Hey, I got something for you, too," he said. He moved his fingers in the air and created a heart-shaped bubble the size of her head. "Tada!"

Emilia snorted and shook her head.

"Dork," she said, and she popped the bubble. Soap specks flew through the air and both stumbled back as it hit them in the eyes.

"Ahh! My eyes!" they cried in unison.

"Come on guys, stop messing around," Mori called from further down the hall.

"Oh yeah, my eyes are immune to soap," said Scuba, opening his. "You okay, Emilia?"

"I'm blind forever," said Emilia sarcastically, though she was smiling.

"Here, I'll help you to the library," said Scuba, grabbing her shoulders and pushing her on down the hall.

"Ahhh I don't trust this!" Emilia exclaimed, still trying to rub at her eyes while stumbling forward.

They gathered in the library and plowed ahead in their decoding attempts, with no success yet again. Scuba was despairing that they would never crack it, and Gloria couldn't blame him. The secret messages were infuriating.

A few weeks later, though, she grew excited as she sensed a breakthrough. A pattern in the code was coming out, she might be able to decode it. Identifying vowels, and working for hours together, they managed to make out most of one of the messages:

"I _onde_ if t_ey k_ow t_ese a_e fake yet."

Mori stared at it a long time, then scowled deeply.

"It says, 'I wonder if they know these are fake yet'," he growled. "He's been messing with us this whole time!"

Scuba stood and walked over to the corner, where he sat down and groaned loudly. Gloria laid her head on the table.

"I can't believe this," she grumbled.

Emilia's hair and arms erupted into flames.

"I... think I should step out to the bathroom a minute," Emilia snarled, then stormed out of the room before anything could catch fire.

"I really hate that guy," said Mori, snatching up the papers and crumbling them up to throw away. "I really, really hate him."

"I can't believe this," Gloria said again, sitting up and shaking her head. "I cannot believe how much time we wasted on this!"

"We have been doing extra math for no reason!" Scuba complained from his corner.

"Worse, we've been distracted from whatever clues we could have gathered on what he's actually planning to do," said Mori, roughly shoving the papers into a wastebasket. "He's been leading us around in circles with these stupid papers, and for all we know, he could have the whole school rigged to blow and we'd never see it coming."

Gloria gripped her pen so tightly it looked like it would snap.

"Even when we were on guard, he figured out how to play us," she said softly. "Dang. We really have to up our game."

The fire alarm went off, lights flashing and sirens blaring to signal them to evacuate. Mori startled at the sound then pinched the bridge of his nose in a frustrated gesture.

"I think that's Emilia," he said.

"Ya think?" Scuba said. He got up slowly to head out, clearly not about to get over all the extra math any time soon.

"Well," Gloria said, grabbing her bag. "Let's go. We can figure out what to do when we regroup."

They headed out to the front lawn where everyone was evacuating to. They could see Emilia sitting by herself a fair distance from the other students, still on fire and glaring fiercely at the withering grass beneath her. A teacher came over and dumped a bucket of water over her, which only created a lot of steam.

In the end, Emilia was sent home until she could "cool off" and everyone else went back inside. They didn't see her until the next day when she came to school beaming with pride as students flooded her with congratulations. Apparently, the day before, Emilia and Gloria's parents had worked together to rescue twenty out of twenty-three hostages held at a prominent local bank. Gloria received the same praise from her classmates, and as a result was a little late meeting up at lunch that day.

CHAPTER FOURTEEN

"Congrats to your parents," said Mori with a grin as the two girls sat. "I'm sure you haven't heard that enough today."

"You know, having superhero parents working all the time can be a real pain," said Emilia with a sigh. "But days like today make it all worth it."

"I can't argue there," Gloria agreed. She'd been feeling a warm wave of contentment washing over her all day, and her cheeks ached from a perpetual smile. "And hey, someday it'll be us doing the rescuing."

"Yeah," said Emilia. "And then our kids will have great days at school and the cycle will continue."

"In the meantime," said Mori, "we should figure out what we're going to do about Carter and Alexandria. I mean, has anyone else noticed that Alexandria didn't show up to school today?"

"Yeah, I haven't seen her anywhere," Scuba said. "And Carter seems....more moody than usual."

"I'll ask around," said Emilia. "I know some girls who keep their ears out for what's what. Maybe they know something."

"Great," said Mori. "On the bright side, if Carter is in a bad mood, hopefully, that means things aren't going well for whatever he's been up to."

"Maybe he's annoyed that our parents saved the day at the bank," said Emilia with a smirk. "Any win for the good guys is an indirect loss for the bad guys, right?"

"Hm, yeah," Gloria said. "We'll have to keep an eye out for sure."

And keep an eye out they did, though nothing really seemed to happen. Emilia's friends didn't come back with the information on why

Alexandria was missing until the day after next, at which time Emilia was ponderously silent at the lunch table.

"Cat got your tongue?" Scuba asked, attempting to steal the cookie from her tray in the process. "What's up, Emilia?"

Emilia snatched the cookie away before he could grab it. "Well... I found out why Alexandria hasn't been at school," said Emilia. "Her parents died. Turns out they were two of the three casualties at the bank."

"Oh," Scuba said, his grin fading. "That's heavy."

"Yeah," said Emilia. "I mean.... She's not exactly citizen of the year or anything, but... that's rough, you know?"

"Yeah," Scuba said.

"I wouldn't come back to school, either," Gloria said.

"Do you think... it wasn't an accident?" said Emilia. "I mean, I'm not saying our parents intentionally tried to kill anybody or get anyone killed, but... I mean you have to wonder where Alexandria got it, all the villain stuff. Maybe her parents weren't just civilians?"

They were silent for a moment as the group digested this thought.

"I dunno," Gloria said finally. "I mean, you've got a point...."

"Yikes," Scuba said, shaking his head.

"You could always ask your parents," said Mori. "I mean, if anyone would know, they would."

"I guess," said Emilia, looking rather uncomfortable at the suggestion.

"Maybe...." Gloria said with equal hesitation.

"Well, I'm sure it wasn't intentional, anyway," said Mori. "I wouldn't worry too much about it."

Emilia nodded, though she definitely still looked worried.

"I wonder how this'll affect their plans, then," Gloria said. "Maybe delay it? Or, I guess maybe not...."

"Yeah, might make them want to act sooner," Scuba said. "That's just what we need."

"We already know Alexandria is easily provoked," said Mori. "Carter tends to do things in a long-term planning sort of way, but he definitely might move his plans up if Alexandria is riled up enough."

Gloria sighed.

"Well, when she comes back, we'll have to be careful," Gloria said.

That evening, Emilia went home to her empty house and waited for her parents to come home. As always, when they did, they were tired from a long day's work, her dad carrying takeout that they'd picked up on the way home.

"Hey... save any more banks today?" said Emilia with a smile.

"No," said Mrs. Marks, flopping down onto the couch and grabbing a carton of Chinese food. "No, we didn't."

"Oh," said Emilia. "Well... I was just sort of wondering about the bank thing... about the civilians that died..."

"Look, honey, we're not perfect," Mr. Marks cut in. "We did what we could, but we can't always save everyone, alright? Sometimes people just die." He gave something of an irritated sigh. "I'm going to take a shower." He stood and marched off to the master bedroom, and Emilia quietly took her share of the Chinese takeout and slipped away to her room.

CHAPTER FIFTEEN

The next day, Alexandria came to school with hot fury in her eyes. Everyone scattered out of her way, by now having heard about why she'd been gone and the circumstances surrounding it. She almost seemed to be casting a dark, foreboding aura around herself.

By the time the first class had started, however, word got around that she and Carter had vanished. This made Gloria anxious, and she had a hard time paying attention to the lesson. Then, the fire alarms went off, making Emilia jump in her seat.

"It's not me!" she exclaimed, further startling Scuba and Gloria next to her. Then, the teacher's computer, the overhead projector, and the phones of the students nearest to the door all flew out into the hallway, attaching themselves to a large, mechanized monstrosity, some sort of mechanical demon, that was now walking down the halls and growing with every classroom it passed.

There were cries of alarm heard from every classroom, and Dr. Vile's name was shouted.

Gloria sprang to her feet, running out of the room without waiting for the teacher or the others. Emilia and Scuba followed, and Mori met them in the halls.

"Is there anything we can do to stop it?" said Mori.

"I can stop it," Emilia growled. She burst into a human ball of flame, then launched herself at the mechanized giant. There was a spark of electricity, and Emilia went flying back, forcing the others to duck as she came hurtling through the air back down the hall like a comet.

"Emilia!" Scuba cried out, and he ran to help her.

"Don't do that again," Gloria called to her, climbing back to her feet. "You'll catch the whole school on fire!"

She scowled, reaching out her hand and sending a blast of wind and sand at the creation, trying to work the tiny particles into its inner workings. The air about the electronic creature fizzled, like some sort of forcefield had formed around it. It was getting further now as well, so big now that it ripped a hole in the wall on its way out rather than squeezing through the door. Ahead of it, they could hear Alexandria blasting things.

"We're too late," said Mori, coming up beside Gloria. "We didn't figure it out in time. We're too late."

"No kidding," Gloria said bitterly. Through the gaping hole in the wall, they could hear Alexandria and Carter laughing.

Part Two:

Villains

CHAPTER SIXTEEN

Alexandria tapped her heels on the legs of the chair, her feet dangling above the linoleum. Her mom was doing paperwork with the lady at the desk, and Alexandria was bored.

She turned in her seat to look out the window, examining the playground from afar. First grade. It sounded so exciting, like the beginning of an adventure. All the other kids had started a month ago, but her family had been moving. Finally, all the boxes had arrived and been taken off of trucks and into the house. Today was the day, she finally got to go to her new school.

"Alright, have fun, Alexandria," her mom said, finally standing. She smiled down at Alexandria. "I'll see you after school."

Alexandria gave her mom a quick hug before running to follow the secretary to her classroom. The teacher, a tall woman with square glasses, had Alexandria introduce herself before she could sit down at her desk in the front of the room. She didn't usually get nervous, but looking out at all of the other kids' faces, she was struck by how unfamiliar they all were.

She couldn't focus on them as she spoke, so her gaze wandered up to the ceiling, across the colorful posters on the wall, and finally to the floor. She twisted the hem of her shirt in her hands, mumbling something about where she was from until the teacher finally told her she could have a seat.

Sitting in the front just made her feel like they were all staring at the back of her head. She was relieved when the lunch bell rang, and she grabbed her lunch box and headed for the cafeteria.

The cafeteria was a loud, chaotic mess of students standing and shouting conversation to one another. They would stand in a clumpy mess that was probably supposed to be a line to get food. Those coming out of the line had to squeeze between tables that had been set up too close together, so getting into a seat took unexpected amounts of planning and coordination.

One boy, sitting not too far from the entrance, noticed her hesitation and her pre-packed lunchbox, and excitedly waved for her to join him. He had dark brown hair cut just a little too short and bright, blue eyes whose energy was only rivaled by his smile.

Alexandria slipped out of the crowd of other kids and sat down across from the boy.

"Hi," she said. "I'm Alexandria."

"I'm Carter," he said. "Nice lunchbox."

"Thanks," Alexandria said, smiling as she clicked it open. It was hot pink, with glitter infused in the plastic. The outside was plastered with the beginnings of her sticker collection. Carter's eyes lingered on the lunchbox.

"I just have a paper sack right now," said Carter. "My dad is making me a lunchbox, but he got a lot of orders so he's going to finish it tonight. He makes costumes."

"Cool. Mine's from the store," Alexandria said. She pulled out her sandwich and took a bite. "What kind of costumes does he make?"

"He makes stuff for superheroes," said Carter. He turned away from her and started unpacking his own paper bag. His held carrot sticks, a sandwich, and a milk carton. "He's really good at it, too."

"That's awesome," Alexandria said. "I'm going to be a superhero someday."

"Oh cool, me too," said Carter with a smile. "Do you have any superpowers?"

"Well, not yet," Alexandria said with a shrug. She wasn't about to let a little thing like that get in her way. "My mom says only some people get them when they're little, a lot of them come when you're older."

"I don't have any yet, either," said Carter, now speaking with his mouth full of peanut butter and jelly sandwich. "But I really hope I get one."

"I hope I can fly," Alexandria said. "And then I'll wear a cape. A pink one," she added decisively.

"Me too," said Carter. "Capes are the best." He roughly swallowed the last of his sandwich. "I mean, every costume looks ten times cooler with a cape on it. No matter what powers I get, I want a cape."

"Unless you have water powers," Alexandria said. "Then it's stupid." Alexandria abandoned the crusts of her sandwich and sifted through the remainder of her lunch. She quickly discarded a baggie of carrot sticks in favor of dessert.

"Well, it could be a waterproof cape," said Carter. "Or maybe fins or something like that." He pulled out his own carrots. "Don't you like carrots? I'll eat them if you don't want them."

Alexandria wrinkled her nose and stuck out her tongue.

"You can have them," she said, pushing the carrots across the table.

Carter bounced excitedly in his seat and piled them into his bag. "My dad says that if you eat lots of carrots, then you might get supervision someday. Other vegetables can give you stuff like super strength and super speed, like apples make you heal faster."

Alexandria eyed him over her lunchbox, chewing her cookie slowly.

"I don't know about that," she said. "Wouldn't more people have superpowers?"

"Very few people actually eat all of their vegetables," said Carter solemnly. He started on his carrots. "My dad says that people hide them under the table and in napkins and stuff, so they never get it. He did that as a kid, which is why he never got any powers."

"Hm," Alexandria said. She still wasn't sure about this method. She would have to ask her cousin Candy about it. Candy was nine, and she knew everything about the 'secret codes' grown-ups used to get kids to do things. "Well, okay."

After finishing his carrots, Carter pulled a container of curry from his sack. "I bet you if I eat lots of really spicy stuff, I'll get fire powers."

"Now that I believe," Alexandria said with a grin. "But only if you don't burn your tongue off first."

"That's what milk is for," said Carter, pointing to his already unpacked milk carton. "I'm going to eat the curry super fast, then drink the milk, and I'll hardly feel it." He took a deep breath, then dug in, shoveling the spicy curry into his mouth.

Alexandria watched with wide eyes, trying not to laugh at him. He was kind of crazy, that she was sure of. But it was a fun kind of crazy.

Soon, lunch was over and they returned to class. Alexandria wished she was sitting next to Carter, and also not in the front. Maybe she could fix that tomorrow.

The next morning, Alexandria raced into the school to look for Carter. She saw him in the hall ahead of her and shouted for him to wait up.

When she caught up to him, she dropped her backpack on the ground and spun around to show off her new, sparkly pink cape.

"Tada!" Alexandria said. "Look what I got!"

"Wow," he breathed, his eyes widening. "That's so cool. I didn't know we could wear capes in school."

"No rule says I can't," Alexandria said proudly. Her mom had checked for her after she begged. "My cousin helped me get it yesterday, she was helping us unpack."

"Wow," he said again. "Can I touch it?"

"Sure," Alexandria said. She grabbed the end of it in her hand and held it out towards him. "Oh, and I asked her about the vegetable thing too. That's why I got this, she said this was better. Visualization," she said the word slowly, she had practiced getting it right. "It's where you tell the universe you want something, and when you tell it enough, you get it. That's what I'm gonna do."

Carter rubbed the corner of the fabric between his fingers. "It's made of rayon, that's cool," he said. He looked up and smiled as an idea struck him. "Hey, maybe I should try that visi-thing, then I'll be twice as likely to get some really cool powers."

"Yeah," Alexandria agreed with a smile. She spun around again, admiring the glittering fabric. "I figured this should get my message across to the universe pretty well. What do you think?"

"I think the universe will give you super cool powers," said Carter. "With lots of sparkles."

Alexandria grinned, then picked her backpack up to head to the classroom.

"Great," she said. "Hey, let's sit together."

"Okay," said Carter, walking with her. He sat to the side of the classroom, closer to the back than the front. Alexandria sat down at the next desk over and hugged her backpack to her chest with one arm as she took out her notebook and pencils. On her other side, a pair of light-haired boys sat down. One had a t-shirt with a dinosaur on it, the other wore a red shirt with a basketball logo on it.

"It's not Halloween, you know," said the basketball boy.

"I know," Alexandria said.

"So why are you dressed like a fairy?" said the other boy.

"I'm not," Alexandria said, frowning. "This is a superhero cape."

"You look like a dumb fairy," said the dinosaur-shirt boy. "Why are you dressed up like that if it isn't Halloween?"

"Um...I just...like capes," Alexandria said, twisting her pencil in her fingers. The dinosaur boy smirked, but the teacher came in and called for them to be quiet before more could be said.

Alexandria squirmed in her seat as she tried to pay attention. Her cape wasn't supposed to look like a fairy outfit, and it definitely wasn't supposed to look stupid.

The boys were back at recess, still trying to tease her about looking like a fairy. Alexandria hurried past them with Carter, on the way to the monkey bars. She tried to ignore them, but by the next day, she was starting to worry. Maybe they were right. Maybe a cape wasn't the best way to go about things.

On Friday, she came to school with her cape tucked in her backpack, zipped out of sight. On her way to class, Carter ran up to her wearing his own, bright red cape with a high pointed collar.

"Hey, look what my dad made me," he said. He dropped his backpack and held up the corners of the cape to show it off. "Cape buddies!" His expression faltered. "Hey, where's yours?"

"Uh...in my backpack," Alexandria admitted. "Aren't you worried it looks kind of....stupid?"

"No," said Carter, a bit confused. "I mean, superheroes don't look stupid. And you looked really cool, so it should work for me, right? I mean, it doesn't have sparkles, but it has this cool collar to keep my neck warm, and it has a little button inside to button it up with if it's windy, see?" He pulled back the collar a bit to show a button.

"That is cool," Alexandria said. "I mean, I didn't think yours looked stupid, I just- well, I can't let you be cool without me now." She smiled and slid off her backpack, digging around until she pulled out her cape.

Carter cheered. "Now we're a superhero team," he said. "Like the ones on the news. Wanna race me to class?"

Alexandria had just finished tying her cape around her neck, and she felt taller as she sprinted towards the classroom. Her backpack swung madly by her heels as she dragged it along.

"You're gonna lose!" she called over her shoulder.

"No way!" he called back, chasing after her with his backpack hugged to his chest. Their capes billowed out behind them as they ran, and they nearly ran directly into dinosaur and basketball.

"Hey! You almost hit me!" the dinosaur boy exclaimed.

"Sorry," said Carter. "Excuse us." He pushed past them to get into the classroom.

"Hey!" the basketball boy protested, though Carter didn't stop. Alexandria was right behind him, and they shoved their way past the boys so they nearly fell into the classroom.

"Sorry," Carter repeated and took the lead back to their desks. The boys followed.

"Why are you wearing a cape?" said basketball boy, crossing his arms.

"Because I'm going to be a superhero," said Carter.

"No you're not, you don't have powers," said dinosaur boy. "And you don't look like a superhero, you look like a vampire."

"I don't think so," said Carter. "But you can pretend if you want; vampires are cool too." He turned to pull out his notebook and pencils, assuming the conversation to be over. The boys looked about to argue, but then the teacher came in and everyone rushed to their seats.

Alexandria smiled and pulled out her notebook. She was glad Carter had a cape too, it made wearing hers even more fun.

On the first day of junior high, Carter missed school without warning. Nobody answered when Alexandria called their home, and none of the teachers knew why he was absent. Finally, when Alexandria called Carter's cell phone during lunch, his father answered and said Carter was in the hospital, having burned his mouth and throat with a dangerously hot chili pepper.

At first, Alexandria didn't quite believe him. After being convinced, and subsequently assured he would be alright, she laughed uncontrollably until she managed to end the phone call.

She had hung her cape in her locker now, it was a bit too cumbersome to wear to every class, but she wasn't ready to let up on the universe. She was still determined to get powers, however long it took. Even so, she had never been very sold on Carter's food method.

Alexandria biked over to the Hospital where Carter was as soon as school ended, and started laughing again before she even found him. Just thinking about it was hilarious, she should have expected this sooner.

As she approached the hospital room, she could hear Carter and his dad arguing, though Carter's voice was raspier and harder to make out.

"You should have told me earlier, then the burning wouldn't have been so bad," Mr. Greys.

"I didn't want you to know I'm an idiot," Carter rasped.

"I already know you're an idiot, it's genetic!" Mr. Greys exclaimed, then stopped when he saw Alexandria through the open door. "Oh hey, nice to see you, Alexandria."

"You too, Mr. Greys," Alexandria said. She looked at Carter, then doubled over laughing once again. "Oh man," she gasped out once it had subsided, "there is no way the universe is giving you fire powers now."

"Well, I think it's safe to assume that much," said Mr. Greys, now smiling in spite of himself. "Apparently the system shock from the pepper brought out his powers."

"I'm a technopath!" said Carter in a breathy cheer, raising his hands into the air. His fingers sparked faintly and the hospital bed jolted, trying to fold up in a quick jerk and startling Carter.

Alexandria snorted, then crossed her arms and gave Carter a stern look.

"Alright, now this is just rude," she said. "You were not supposed to get powers before me!"

"Sorry," said Carter, though he clearly wasn't, despite the injuries. "You'll get 'em soon, though. Apparently, vegetables don't make powers, though late bloomers tend to get it with puberty and stuff."

"I always told you the food thing was dumb," Alexandria said, shaking her head. But she was smiling. "Anyway, if you get powers and I don't, I swear I'll never forgive you."

"Aw, you know that won't happen," said Carter. "I just cheated by almost dying by chili pepper."

"And 'the food thing' wasn't dumb, it was genius," said Mr. Greys. "You saw how many vegetables he ate; I should get a parenting award."

"Sure, I mean, it also landed us here," Alexandria said with a shrug, "but that's really Carter's fault. Anyway, I gotta get to gymnastics." She slung her backpack over her shoulder and turned to Carter. "Don't eat anything else dumb."

"Just yogurt," said Carter with a sad croak. "And jello."

"Have fun, Alexandria," said Mr. Greys. "I'll let you know when Carter's released home."

"Thanks," Alexandria said with a smile, then she left, still shaking her head in amusement.

After that incident, Carter didn't return to school. His father pulled him out to be homeschooled while he learned to control his new powers out of range of the school's computers, phones, calculators, and other electronic devices. This proved a wise decision after he wrecked his gaming console when he and Alexandria were playing on it after school, frying the whole system and the TV during a jumpscare. After that, they found non-electronic based activities like reading and board games, and Carter never stopped wearing his cape.

CHAPTER SEVENTEEN

It had been a torturously long two months after Carter got his powers before she got hers, but her negotiating with the universe had finally paid off. After that, it was just a matter of waiting until they were 15, old enough to go to this school.

Alexandria scanned the cafeteria quickly before finding a place to sit. It was the first day at the special high school for future heroes, and no matter what Carter said, she was definitely the more excited one. They had been wanting to go here for so long, it was almost hard to believe they were actually there. She didn't see Carter yet, but she figured he'd turn up soon enough.

Alexandria spotted Emilia, a girl she had met in class earlier, and headed over to sit with her.

"I mean, it's like foreshadowing, except in life," Gloria was saying. Gloria was tall and had dark hair and skin, her eyes a light brown that almost looked gold. She sounded like she'd just made a point as Alexandria walked up. "It'll probably be even more obvious in hindsight, if you think about it."

"Hey, what are you guys talking about?" Alexandria asked, sliding into the bench next to Emilia.

"Oh, hey, Alexandria," said Emilia. "We were just talking about the guy over there, totally going to be a supervillain, am I right?" Emilia pointed across the cafeteria to where Carter was walking toward one of the tables near the door, his brand new, high-collared, black and blue cape billowing behind him. His pale eyes were brighter now, an electric blue that had developed after his powers came in, and he had a couple of small gadgets on his belt.

Alexandria snorted. "Carter? Nah, trust me, there's no way."

Mori, a kid with black hair and dark eyes, looked at Alexandria from Gloria's other side. "He's in my science class," he said. "He nearly blew up the lab. It made a mushroom cloud, Alexandria, like those scary cartoon ones."

Alexandria rolled her eyes. The idea of Carter being a supervillain was funny enough to be part of a stand-up comedy routine, she thought.

"Probably an accident, he's no good at chemistry," Alexandria said. "But being bad at science isn't exactly evil."

Over at the table by the door, Carter laughed loudly at something one of the other boys said, and the lights in the ceiling above him flickered and buzzed, then a thin bolt of electricity leaped down and shocked one of the boys off his seat. Emilia gave Alexandria a pointed look, her hand extended toward the scene.

"Yeah, how do you explain that?" Another boy, Scuba, asked. Scuba was tall, but not in the same way as Gloria, more gangly than anything.

"Okay…" Alexandria said, a bit hesitantly. That dork, he was going to get in trouble if he didn't get his powers under control. "I mean, he's a clutz and a technopath. His powers are pretty closely tied to his emotions. Especially his laughter emotion. So, you know, probably an accident…?"

"Laughter isn't an emotion, Alexandria," said Emilia, rolling her eyes. "I mean, fireballs don't blow up behind me when I laugh. My powers don't do anything when I laugh, only when I'm angry or upset."

"So his powers are more fun," Alexandria said with a shrug. She bit into her sandwich. Don't overreact, she told herself, play it cool and shoot for a change of subject. "Seriously, you want a different candidate for villain speculating, once you get to know him, you'll realize it's ridiculous."

"Unless he's manipulating you," Mori muttered into his milk carton. Alexandria's head snapped around to stare down Mori. That was uncalled for.

"Excuse me?" Alexandria said. Her raised eyebrows clearly told him he was getting a chance to rephrase the statement.

"Well, I mean, it's a thing that psychopaths do; they act likable and nice to manipulate people," said Mori. "And anyway, technopaths are statistically more likely to be supervillains, and when you combine that with how he dresses…" Mori glanced over at Carter. "Well, it's kind of weird that they let him into the school in the first place, when you really think about it."

"Okay, seriously, this started kind of funny, but now it's just getting rude," Alexandria said. "Talk about being judgemental." She shook her head in disgust.

"I'm not being judgemental," said Mori, irritably. "I'm just saying that he falls into a certain profile. It's not my fault that you're intent on ignoring it."

"Falling into a profile does not disqualify you from going to school," Alexandria said. "Especially when you haven't done anything wrong. And he's not a psychopath, either."

"I dunno," Gloria said, though her tone suggested she did know, "I think Mori has a point. I mean... he just zapped a guy."

At the table by the door, the group of boys that Carter had sat by were moving away, some leaving and some pretending to before going to another table, leaving Carter sitting alone. Alexandria sighed, then got up.

"It was probably an accident," she repeated with a hard tone, "and I'm not hungry anymore." She left and dumped what was left of her food into the trash on her way out.

She didn't get far before Carter caught up with her.

"Hey, leaving already?" he said.

"Yeah," Alexandria said. "I lost my appetite."

"Hm, cafeteria food will do that," said Carter. "Want some of mine? It's packed from home, complete with 55% less food poisoning." He gestured grandly to his lunchbox like it was a new car. Alexandria laughed.

"Sure, thanks," she said.

They found a place to sit in the hall, and Carter laid out what was left of his lunch, which was still most of it. There was a sandwich, which he split in half and took the bitten part for himself, an apple, a juice box, and a cookie. He gave the cookie to Alexandria and launched into the narrative of how he'd nearly blown up the chemistry lab.

"It was like a sign from nature," said Carter. He held his hands in the air to frame an imaginary sign. "Carter must not do chemistry."

"How do you even make a mistake that bad?" Alexandria asked as she poked him in the shoulder. "I probably couldn't if I tried."

"With great incompetence comes great explosions," said Carter. "That's something my dad and I came up with when I was homeschooled. Though apparently, things blow up in Mrs. Reed's lab all the time. She has potential energy powers, so things around her tend to be more combustible than they otherwise would be."

"Yeah, good thing, otherwise you could have gotten kicked out of class for something like that," Alexandria said, elbowing him in the ribs. Maybe she wouldn't even tell Carter what the other kids had been saying, she thought, it wouldn't do any good anyway. People were just stupid. "Just stick to your electronics." She paused. "But don't zap people, moron." She smacked his arm.

"Ow!" he grimaced and rubbed his arm. "It wasn't my fault, that kid had braces, and the seats were metal. He was a ridiculously good conductor, and I'm…"

"Going to apologize later, right?" she said pointedly.

"Yeah…" said Carter. "He is fine though, and his expression was really funny. Anyway, how's your day been?"

"Pretty good," Alexandria said. "Nothing that exciting for me. Only lunch has been less enjoyable so far."

"Yeah, the food's the worst," said Carter. "You're not the only one who bailed early on a foul stomach, I lost my whole table to it. Well, except the kid who had a club meeting, but anyway, my dad's friend used to go here. That's how I got the heads up and got a home lunch." He grinned. "Speaking of my dad, what do you think of the new cape? I figure visualization isn't just for grade school." He winked.

"I like it," Alexandria said, now smiling a bit. "Maybe I'll break out the pink glitter monster again. It'd go with my lunchbox." Out of the corner of her eye, she saw Gloria shake her head at her. Alexandria pointedly ignored her.

"That'd be the best," said Carter, laughing. "Man, honest truth here, I was so jealous of your cape as a kid. I wouldn't leave my dad alone until he made me mine." He glanced at where Gloria had disappeared around the corner. "Make any new friends here?"

"Hm, maybe, it's under review," Alexandria said. "I thought I had, but…..well, they might not be a good fit after all. We'll see."

"Yeah, I know the feeling," said Carter. "My lab partner, this guy Mori, wasn't much for having such a…. an attention-grabbing guy like me and my fantastic cape sitting by him. He's a seriously shy guy, though I think people will get over it quick enough. I mean, this is a school for heroes, after all, they're going to have to get used to capes at some point."

"Yeah," Alexandria said. "I met Mori, too. He didn't seem like one of the better prospects, honestly."

"Really?" said Carter. "I would have thought you two would already be friends. You've met him before, right?"

"Uh, no, just today," Alexandria said. "Anyway, he's just an idiot. Bit narrow-minded. But you're his lab partner, you can probably win him over. Especially if you try not to blow up his homework or something," Alexandria gave him a pointed look, though it was ruined by her grin.

"Yeah yeah, we already made an arrangement," said Carter, waving his hand dismissively. "I do the physics-type stuff, he does the chemistry. That way we both get an A and nobody gets blown up."

"That's good," Alexandria said. She thought of Mori's remarks earlier and shook her head slightly.

"So what'd he do to get on your bad side?" said Carter, "if you don't mind me asking."

"Ah, just being an idiot," Alexandria said with a shrug. "Him and some others. I guess he was still upset about the explosion or something. They were just going on about you, actually, becoming a villain or something."

Carter laughed. "Me? A villain? That'll last, what with my naturally terrifying personality and all. My first evil plan will be to set the outrageous trend of high-collared capes."

"I know, I laughed too," Alexandria said, smiling slightly. "I thought it was pretty funny. But they wouldn't let it go, it got pretty annoying."

"Ah, I'm guessing that's what got your stomach, then?" said Carter.

"Yeah," Alexandria admitted. So, not telling him hadn't worked out. That figured, she couldn't remember the last time she kept anything other than a Christmas present a secret from him.

"Well, thanks for sticking up for me," said Carter. "You're a good friend, you know that?"

"Ah, anytime," Alexandria said. She elbowed him and added, "I try to set people straight when they don't realize you're actually a total dork."

"Gee, thanks," said Carter. He stuck his thumbs behind the hems of his cape by his chest. "Don't worry, I'll set them straight soon enough."

"I'm sure you will," Alexandria said.

The bell rang, startling Carter so hard that his phone on his belt started playing mariachi music. He frantically turned it off.

"Well, I think that's our cue for class," said Carter. "See you later, yeah?"

"Yeah, see you after class," Alexandria said, getting up to leave. Carter gathered up his things and headed to his next class.

CHAPTER EIGHTEEN

After going through all of his classes and seeing who was in what with him, Carter made his move in his history class, coming to sit right between Gloria and Scuba. He had to gather up his cape to make sure it didn't spill out over on top of his and their backpacks, though he gave them both friendly smiles as he did so.

"Hey, I'm Carter," he said.

"Hey," Gloria said, giving him a quick once-over before turning back to her book. "Gloria."

"Nice to meet you, Gloria," said Carter. He glanced over at Scuba, he remembered his name from roll call. "And you're Scuba, right?"

"Yeah, that's me," Scuba said with a smile. "So.....what's with the cape?"

"It's cool, and it keeps my neck warm when I button up the collar," said Carter. "I've already figured out how to use my power for flying, so I figure wind and all that is going to be a factor."

"It's definitely got the vampire vibe," Gloria said. "You know, dark and brooding or whatever."

"I don't know about that," said Carter, "it feels more warm and cozy to me, but I guess everyone has their own style. What about you guys? Any costume ideas yet?"

"Eh, a few," Scuba said with a shrug. "I mean, I've got bubbles. I make bubbles out of soap, and I soak the soap through my skin. So we'll see. Gloria, though, she's got it all figured out."

"Oh?" said Carter, somewhat stunned by Scuba's description of his powers as he turned to look at Gloria. "What do you have planned?"

"Something I've been working on a while," Gloria said with a smug smile. "You'll have to wait and see just like everyone else."

"Fair enough," said Carter. "Well, I could help you out, Scuba, if you want. My dad does a lot of costume design, and I'm pretty good at coming up with extra tricks for super suits."

"Ah, I'll figure it out," Scuba said. He smiled nervously, like everything he said was a roll of social dice.

"Suit yourself," said Carter with a grin. Scuba groaned exaggeratedly and shook his head.

"That was so punny it hurt," Scuba said.

"Ah yes, puns, my true superpower," said Carter. "Speaking of which, what are you guys doing after school? I was thinking we could practice our powers a bit together, you know? So if things ever come up, we'll already know each other's powers and things really well. Easier for teaming up and all that."

Gloria shot a hard to interpret look at Scuba. An indecisive debate flashed across Scubas face as he prepared to roll the dice once more.

"Well, yeah, sounds like a good idea," Scuba said after a moment.

"Great," said Carter. "Where do you want to meet up?"

"There's a field past the football field we could use," Gloria suggested.

"That works," said Carter. He pulled out his phone to text Alexandria. "Mind if I invite a friend?"

"Alexandria, right?" Gloria asked. She shrugged, "Yeah, sure."

"Great," said Carter. He shot her the text with the details, then quickly stuffed the phone away as the teacher entered and the class hushed.

CHAPTER NINETEEN

Carter and Alexandria hiked out to the field together. Carter lugged a large wagon full of electronic parts and materials, things he'd gotten from his dad and from the dump. Alexandria noticed the group, more than she'd expected from what Carter had said, watching them apprehensively. Her stomach tightened; she hoped Carter wouldn't mess this up for himself. He really could use more friends.

"Okay, promise me you'll try and be cool, okay?" said Alexandria. "Don't do anything embarrassing."

"Ah, me? Embarrassing?" Carter asked, grinning. "I'll try."

"Hey," said Gloria as they got close enough to hear without shouting.

"Hey," said Carter, trying to act cool. "I see you brought the rest of your friends. That should make things more interesting."

Alexandria tried not to grimace. Now he was trying too hard. He was doomed; she'd be his only friend forever.

"Yeah," Gloria said, looking somewhat confused.

"Well," said Carter, clapping his hands together, nervously trying to change the subject. "Why don't we see how well we can travel together?" He glanced about the group. "I figure a good number of us can fly, but Mori… will probably need some help."

"Alright, well, I can probably help Mori out," said Gloria, a bit quickly. Were they dating?

"Thanks," said Mori, smiling at her. Yep, definitely dating.

"Great, so that's Mori taken care of," said Carter. He waved his hand, sending tendrils of electricity flying from his fingertips to snatch up the materials he'd brought in his wagon. The gears and wires and metal parts all floated up, swirling about him in the air a moment before assembling as his mind directed, creating a metal platform with some sort of engine beneath it. Alexandria watched it with a smile, watching with a pleasant sense of wonder as the parts moved over their heads and into their places. She always forgot how amazing his power was until she saw it. The platform landed at their feet, and Carter let his hand drop.

"I can take people on this," Carter said, gesturing to the platform. He glanced briefly at the others. Could they all fly?

"Well, I can already fly," said Emilia, crossing her arms defensively under his gaze. "So that just leaves Alexandria, really."

"I'll ride with Carter," Alexandria said without hesitation. "I definitely can't fly."

"That's everyone, then," said Emilia. She rolled her shoulders, somewhat aggressively.

Carter stepped onto his platform with Alexandria, and the machine crackled with his electricity as parts shifted to lock about their feet to hold them into position. Then the engine hummed and the platform hovered upward a few inches. The vibration tickled the soles of Alexandria's feet.

"Let's do one lap around the field," said Carter. "Try to keep close and figure out some kind of formation, yeah?"

"Yeah, sounds cool," said Scuba. As the others took off, Scuba remained on the ground, focusing, before shooting past Carter and Alexandria in a giant bubble.

"Wow," Carter said to Alexandria. The others couldn't hear them over the distance and the hum of the engine. "It's like the Wizard of Oz."

"Careful, he might drop a house on us," said Alexandria with a snicker. Maybe they all would get along after all. Scuba, at least, seemed like Carter's level of dork.

They kept a fair distance from the others, though not intentionally. From the somewhat intense expression on Carter's face, Alexandria could tell he was focusing rather hard to keep the whole thing together.

"Remind me to practice hovercrafts more," said Carter. "This, ah, is my first one."

"What!?" Alexandria hissed. "I swear, if you drop us-" she was interrupted by a large spark in the workings beneath their feet, and a screw launched itself out of the platform and popped Scuba's bubble.

Alexandria yelped in surprise and grabbed Carter's arm tightly, making the whole thing veer slightly before settling.

"Carter!" she exclaimed. She smacked his arm as Scuba managed to catch himself in another bubble. "You almost killed him!"

"It's fine, he's fine, we're fine," said Carter, his eyes wide in the most hilarious expression of frozen terror and concentration. "Look, see? He bounces." Scuba's bubble bounced off the grass below, and Alexandria snorted. As long as everyone was okay, it really was quite hilarious. The expressions on both Carter and Scuba's faces were priceless.

"Don't laugh, that's insensitive," said Carter with the most hilariously serious expression, now smacking her arm. That made her laugh harder as they landed. He turned to face the others, "Well, I think that went well. I mean, obviously my hovercraft could use some work." Scuba was now standing wide-eyed behind Emilia. No, she couldn't laugh! Another snort escaped, and Carter shot her a look before continuing. "But other than that, I think we kept together pretty well."

"Yeah," said Gloria, giving Carter's hovercraft a look. Carter was looking at it too, disappointed that it had worked out so terribly. Well, it flew, at least, but clearly had some design flaws.

"So next," said Carter, clapping his hands together again, eager to change the subject, "let's figure out costumes. I mean, obviously I have something in mind already for myself," he gestured at his flowing black and dark blue cape with the pointed collar. Alexandria smiled at this. He really did love costumes.

"Ah yes, well," said Mori, "I don't think we really need to decide all of that right now."

Carter shook his head. "Gloria will be blowing a lot of dust into the air," he said. "We should wear something to protect our eyes; that'll also help if Gloria has to put up some sort of dust smokescreen, and of course there's nothing worse than getting soap in your eyes." He grinned at Scuba, who almost didn't dare breathe under his gaze.

"Yeah, the last thing we need is to get blinded in the middle of something," Alexandria said. Honestly, she'd hoped they would work on more power-related things, but after the bubble incident, maybe costumes would be safer.

"Alright," Gloria said with a shrug. She and the others looked pretty eager to leave at this point. Poor Carter was too nervous to notice. "So we incorporate eye protection into our costumes."

"I could make some," Carter suggested, "if you-"

Mori cut him off. "Actually, I think we should all make our own," he said, exchanging another glance with Gloria. "Otherwise it might not fit right, you know?"

"Oh, alright," said Carter, frowning somewhat at the suggestion. Alexandria could tell he was disappointed. "Makes sense, I guess."

"I think that covers everything," said Emilia.

"Yeah, I think so," said Gloria with a hurried nod.

"And I have homework to get to," Scuba exclaimed very suddenly.

"Okay…" said Carter. "Well… maybe we can do some more practice like this another time."

"Maybe," said Gloria flatly.

"Bye," said Carter with a halting wave, but they were already gone, scattering away on the field. He glanced at Alexandria.

"Well… I can give you a ride home if you want," he said. "I've already got a hovercraft set up, after all."

"Ah, maybe we should walk," Alexandria said with a grimace.

Carter nodded sadly. "That didn't go well, did it." It wasn't even a question.

"It's alright, it wasn't your fault," said Alexandria. "Come on, you can walk me home."

Carter nodded and glumly gathered up the parts into his wagon before following her off the field.

CHAPTER TWENTY

The next few days showed little activity from the group, at least, they were hard for Carter to get ahold of. Whenever he tried to sit by them at lunch, the table was full, and they always left in a hurry after classes. Sitting by them unexpectedly during class didn't work a second time, either, as they always had people on either side of them when Carter arrived. Finally, Carter asked Alexandria to talk to them.

"I don't know if I did something to offend them," he said, "but I definitely feel like they're avoiding me. Mori even changed lab partners. I tried talking to Emilia in our math class, but she always says she's busy, and I've considered talking to Gloria and Scuba in history, but Gloria keeps glaring at me."

"Hm," Alexandria said. Irritation welled up inside her. One accident on the field and they resort to shunning him? "I'll talk to them, try to see what's going on. Maybe they've just been busy...." she didn't really believe it, but she couldn't think of a good excuse for them, either.

She cornered them before school, but no luck there. They were convinced that Carter was some sort of psychopath and refused to give him a chance to prove otherwise. Of course, this left her in a sour mood that only accumulated as the day went on.

Right before lunch, in Alexandria's English class, a rather large, athletic guy with red hair came to sit by Alexandria. This took her somewhat by surprise, as he was normally rather shy and sat in the back.

"Hi," he said. "I'm Ed, what's your name?"

"Oh, uh, hi," Alexandria said. "Alexandria."

"Cool, nice to meet you," he said. A moment of silence passed, and he bit his lip, looking somewhat nervous. "So... what's your superpower?"

"Oh, energy manipulation," Alexandria said. It had already amused her a bit how long she'd gone without anyone asking, she'd expected it to be a much more common question. "Like, plasma and stuff." She held out her hand, a pink glowing energy around her fingers as an example.

"That's cool," said Ed. He pulled out a notebook and scribbled something down. Alexandria raised an eyebrow.

"Taking notes?" she asked. "What's your superpower?"

"Oh, I just teleport stuff," he said. "Not myself or anything, just little things, like this." He ripped off the piece of paper and, with a flash of green light, it disappeared from his hand. "That was for Mori. He was just wondering what your power is since you're Carter's Harley Quinn and all that."

Alexandria paused with a frown, turning to look at his face.

"I'm sorry, what?"

"You know," said Ed, "Harley Quinn, the Joker's girlfriend sidekick. Carter's a supervillain, like the Joker, and you're his Harley Quinn. It's not a secret, the whole school knows."

Alexandria took a deep breath.

"Alright, let's get something straight," she said. "Carter isn't a supervillain, and besides that, he's my friend, not my employer or whatever the Joker is supposed to be. That's one of the most idiotic things I've heard today, and the bar was already set pretty low, so congratulations. You win the stupid award for the day."

Ed scowled. "Hey, don't get mad at me, I'm just the messenger," he said. "And if you don't want people thinking you work for a supervillain, maybe you should try not hanging out with one."

Alexandria stood suddenly, turning and punching Ed square in the jaw so hard he fell backward out of his seat.

"He's not a villain, he's my friend," she said with a scowl. "And don't call me Harley Quinn."

Ed stood, his hand balling into a fist. The teacher intervened.

"Alexandria, Principal's office, now," she said sharply. Alexandria turned on her heel.

"Feel free to pass that along to Mori when you see him," she said over her shoulder as she left.

CHAPTER TWENTY-ONE

Alexandria was notably absent at lunch, as she was stuck in detention as a result of the English class fiasco, word of which had spread through most of the student body. Carter didn't hear about it, but he knew there was something everyone was talking about, as they shot him covert glances during their conversations. With some hesitation, he went to speak to Gloria and the others at their table.

"Seat's taken," said Mori by instinct as he approached.

"Yeah, I know, I'm looking for Alexandria," said Carter. "Have you seen her?"

"Not since this morning," Gloria said. "And sounds like I should count myself lucky for it."

Carter scowled. "What's that supposed to mean?"

"She decked a guy in English today," Scuba said. "Just blew up at him."

"What? Why? What'd he do?" said Carter. He never thought of Alexandria as the violent type.

"They were talking," Gloria said with a shrug. "But it's not that hard to get her worked up about whatever, is it?"

"Not without good reason," said Carter irritably. "I don't know what your problem is with her; she never did anything to you."

"Well if you don't know, just think it over," Gloria said. "It'll come to you."

"Actually, I don't think it will," said Carter, exasperatedly. Why did this group always insist on playing these games? He was just a normal person, so was Alexandria. Why couldn't they see that?

"Well, for starters, it's not Alexandria that's the real problem," Gloria said. Scuba looked at Carter, then back at his lunch. Carter scowled.

"Oh right, I'd almost forgotten," he said darkly. "You all think I'm some sort of supervillain, right?" The words hurt even coming from his own mouth. "All I've ever done is try to be your friend."

"Which, you know, wasn't that hard to see through," said Mori under his breath.

He thought of Alexandria, in detention for something that was probably their doing. He thought of all the time he'd agonized over trying to gain their approval, trying to be 'cool' yet somehow not whatever monster they thought he was. He could feel his powers burning in his veins.

"Well, if you're all so convinced," he said, glaring at them, "then there's no point in me trying to be nice, now is there?"

The group exchanged glances but didn't respond. Carter's scowl deepened and his fingers sparked with electricity. He wanted to smack them across the face, make them explain what happened to Alexandria, knock some sense into them somehow. But that wouldn't do any good. He turned and stormed away to find Alexandria. Whatever had happened, she was the one that needed him now.

It didn't take him long after that to find out about her detention, which extended to after school as well. He wasn't allowed to see her until she was let out later that afternoon, despite his protests to the teachers. He spent the time brooding and, occasionally, stifling tears. He didn't understand why everyone hated him, why they all were so convinced he was evil. What had he done differently than the rest? He'd come to learn to be a hero, like everyone else, not to be pegged as the next generation's number one most wanted.

He waited outside the detention hall after school until Alexandria came out. When she finally emerged, she was scowling irritably.

"Hey, are you alright?" said Carter, standing.

"Yeah, I'm fine," Alexandria said, glancing over at him. "You?"

"Yeah," said Carter with a sigh. "So... what happened?"

"Well," Alexandria sighed. "I was already in a bad mood after talking to the group this morning, you know. I didn't get a chance to tell you how that went, but it wasn't great. Basically, they all still think you're a psychopath." Alexandria shook her head.

"So, then this guy, Ed, talks to me in English," she continued. "But pretty quickly let's slip that he's just spying for Mori. I was, you know, kinda mad about that, and then he was just being a jerk." She glanced over at Carter. "Apparently we're being compared to the Joker and Harley Quinn. He wouldn't take it back, so I punched him."

Carter's fingers sparked as anger flashed across his face. "I hope it hurt," he said darkly.

"Oh, he'll be feeling it for days," Alexandria said with a satisfied smile.

"Good," said Carter. "I mean, even if I were some sort of psychopath, he'd deserve it for calling you Harley Quinn."

"Thanks," Alexandria said. She sighed, "But it probably didn't help, they probably just feel validated now."

"Well, there doesn't seem to be any way of getting around that," said Carter. "I've been thinking, if anyone in this school is acting like a villain, it's them. So, as aspiring heroes, maybe it's time we dished out some justice."

"You know, I have to agree with you there," Alexandria said. "What do you have in mind?"

"Well, technically, I already did it," Carter admitted. "It's small, but I think it gets the point across. We're in a school for heroes, and they're pretty much failing at acting like heroes. I figured that it would make sense if their grades reflected that." He gestured down the hall to the computer lab. "It's all set in the computers; they should be getting the email from their counselors tomorrow. As per school policy, it'll be sent to their parents as well."

"Ooh, diabolical," Alexandria said with a grin. "I like it."

"Thanks," said Carter. He gave the corners of his collar an arrogant flip. "So, want me to walk you home?"

"Sure," Alexandria said. "Probably better not to risk what I'd do to one of them if I caught them alone."

"Probably," Carter agreed.

CHAPTER TWENTY-TWO

Alexandria was spending most of the next day being avoided by other students. She figured this was better than getting into fights, which looked likely judging by the suspicious glances she was getting. Detention wasn't going to be worth it a second time, she told herself.

In Math that afternoon, they were supposed to work with partners, but even the teacher didn't object when Alexandria didn't try to find one. She opened her book and began the work by herself, her posture making it clear she wasn't available for partnership. Unfortunately, she also shared this class with Ed, and he didn't seem to get the hint.

"So, do you have a partner?" said Ed. He came to stand directly in front of her desk.

"Mori send you to heckle me again?" Alexandria asked without looking up. "Not interested. Move along."

"I'm not heckling," said Ed. "I just don't have a partner."

"And I'm just not interested," Alexandria replied.

"Look, I get that you're into Carter, but that doesn't mean you need to snub every other guy that tries to talk to you," said Ed.

"I'm not snubbing you because I'm into Carter," Alexandria said. "I'm snubbing you because you're a jerk. So are your friends."

"They're not jerks," said Ed. "They're heroes. It's not my fault you can't take the truth when you hear it."

"Funny definition of truth you've got there," Alexandria said bitterly. "Look, we're not evil, and neither of us wants to be villains. Saying it doesn't just make it true. And honestly, if those are the world's future heroes, it's no wonder this world's a mess."

"Did Carter say that, or did you think it up all on your own?" said Ed.

"And what's that supposed to mean?" Alexandria asked, scowling and finally looking up at him.

"I mean that you're Harley Quinn and you're letting Carter mess with your head," said Ed. "Just because you like him, doesn't mean you have to do what he says. There are better guys out there, you know? Guys that don't try to get sympathy by crying in the hallways while they're plotting evil schemes."

"Carter doesn't tell me what to do," Alexandria said. "And I'd really like to see you try to find a better guy, and don't even think of using yourself as an example. Where are you even getting this stuff? Is Mori telling you? Let me tell you, whatever you're up to, it's a bad idea."

"Mori isn't telling me anything," said Ed. "It's just obvious, you know? It's what everybody is saying."

"Well, everyone is stupid, then," Alexandria said. She turned away, looking back at her book and intent on ignoring him. She clenched her fist at her side and resisted the urge to give him a matching shiner on the other side. She would try to be civil, even if the heroes couldn't be bothered to.

"Hey, I'm talking to you," said Ed. When she didn't respond, he teleported her book into his hands.

"Give me my book back," Alexandria said through gritted teeth. "I'm trying to do the classwork."

"I'll give it back when you admit you're a Harley Quinn," said Ed.

"I am not," Alexandria said forcefully. She snatched at the book in Ed's hands. Ed dodged out of her reach, holding the book up high.

"Say it," he repeated. "You'll feel better if you say it. Just admit it, you're Harley Quinn."

Alexandria glared at him. She turned away from him and put her head in her arms resting on her desk. Without her book, she couldn't do the work, but he might at least leave her alone if she ignored him long enough. Ed snapped his fingers about her desk and called her name a few times, then dropped her book on the floor and went back to his desk.

Alexandria waited a moment, then picked up her book and opened it to finish the work. She didn't look at any of the other students or the teacher for the rest of the class period.

On her way out of class, she felt a hand reach out and give her hair a quick tug. Alexandria spun around, furious, shoving the offender away hard.

"Get away from me!" She practically shouted, scowling deeply.

Ed tumbled to the ground, hard, and the teacher's voice barked over the ensuing rumble of student voices.

"Detention, Alexandria!" she barked.

"What?" Alexandria asked, outraged. "Did you see what he did?"

"What I saw was you just shoved Edward to the ground," said the teacher. "That is your second offense against him, at that. Detention, no arguments."

Alexandria shot Ed a poisonous glare before turning on her heel and leaving.

CHAPTER TWENTY-THREE

That afternoon, Carter heard in the halls that, once again, Alexandria had gotten detention from punching Ed. That meant that, once again, Mori and Gloria's gang had sent him to harass her.

His vision burned red and the lights flickered as he passed them. He could barely think, but he knew he had to find the gang, make them stop. He passed through the gym on a shortcut to the other half of the school when he saw Emilia coming the other way.

"There you are!" he snarled. Despite his best efforts, electricity leaped from his fingertips and into the ground around him. He ignored them. He was going to give Emilia a piece of his mind. He opened his mouth again to shout at her, but a wall of flames erupted between him and Emilia. He stumbled back, eyes widening. He redirected his powers to bring down panels from the ventilation shaft above to smother the flames, which were creeping toward him. Gloria, Mori, and Scuba entered just as Carter took a step beyond the rubble.

"Emilia!" Scuba cried out, and suddenly Carter was engulfed in foamy bubbles, pushing him backward. The soap was in his mouth, his nose, and his eyes, burning and making him cough. Then several copies of Mori leaped through the veil of bubbles to tackle him. Carter fought back with everything he had, clawing and sending out waves of electricity to drive back his attackers and the bubbles. He forced his eyes to open despite the burning; he had to see. But he only managed to get them open in time to see Emilia's blazing fist flying at him, slamming into his forearms as he brought them up to protect his face. He threw his arms out and moved aside, letting Emilia fall from her own force, and turned to face the others.

Gloria raised her hands, sending a sandblast to try and knock Carter off his feet. He coughed and covered his eyes as once again they were bombarded, now with rough grains of sand, but stood his ground. Emilia leaped up and cuffed him on the side of the head with another flaming fist and a kick to the leg that sent him staggering before his knees hit the ground. Still, he wasn't done. His hands exploded with electricity, blasting out at the group and causing them to quake with pain.

The air narrowed into a cyclone around Carter, driving the sand into his nose and mouth, getting into his lungs. Then Scuba tackled him from behind, and Carter blasted him with electricity as they fell. He pulled his cape up to shield against the wind and sand that was still spinning in the air around them. He could barely breathe. He couldn't see. He wanted it all to stop.

As the others continued their attack, Carter continued to blast out with electricity, trying to drive them away. Still, the punches, the kicks, and the howling wind and coarse sand continued. His cape burned repeatedly as Emilia fought like a rabid dog, snarling and scratching and bringing fire with every attack.

Then, there was a sickening snap, and there was a brief instant when Carter didn't even feel it yet. Then he screamed in agony. The gang backed off, the dust settled, and Carter lay in place, curled on the ground, screaming and crying from the pain in his arm, his face, his eyes and lungs, and most of all, his leg. He couldn't register anything that happened beyond that pain, and it seemed to hold him for an eternity before finally, as he was lifted onto a stretcher by unseen hands, he blacked out.

CHAPTER TWENTY-FOUR

Alexandria smoothed the fabric in her hands as she stood in the rising elevator. This time, Carter wasn't in the hospital for doing something stupid. No, this time it was someone else's fault. She bit her lip and rubbed her thumb over the button on the collar of the cape.

The black and blue fabric was identical to the old cape, the one that had been destroyed. Alexandria's gut clenched at the thought. The elevator doors slid open and she stepped out into the sterile smelling hallway.

When she stepped into Carter's hospital room, she wrinkled her nose against the hospital smell mixed with a heavy scent of pollen. Flowers of yellow, blue, and violet dotted the window sill, bedside table, and the floor about the door and the bed.

Carter lay still in the bed, his eyes closed and his breathing slow and even. Alexandria bit her lip as she looked at him. She had known it was bad, Mr. Greys had tried to warn her, but the sight of him hit her in the gut like an errant football.

One side of his face was bandaged, for burns, Mr. Greys had said. One arm was in a cast, the other wrapped in layers of gauze. More burns. His broken leg was in a cast and hung suspended gently above the bed. Surgery had taken hours, and Carter had yet to regain consciousness. A feeding tube looped out from his mouth, and an IV dangled from a hanger beside him, connected to a small bare part of his inner arm on the other side of the gauze.

Alexandria draped the folded cape over the bed railing, looking around the room. The flowers were unexpected and she ran a hand through the blossoms as she glanced around at the glitter-laden cards. She picked one up and scowled.

The flowers were some pathetic attempt at an apology. The parents of his attackers, no doubt, were really the ones who were sorry. Suspension, and detention. They should be expelled, they should be barred from hero work forever.

The thoughts boiled in Alexandria's mind and gut. Alexandria slammed the card down on the table. Her hand gripped a bouquet of now shriveled flowers. She tore them out of the vase and threw them at the trashcan, most of the stems scattered on the floor.

"I'm sorry, Carter," Alexandria said, looking back at his sleeping face. It wouldn't look that peaceful once he woke up, not once he had to go back to school.

Alexandria yanked the door open and left, wiping her eyes on her sleeve as she punched the button for the elevator. The medicated smell of the hospital stung her nose.

Carter didn't return to school for several weeks and spent most of that time either sleeping with pain medication or in physical therapy. As a result, she didn't see much of him until he returned to school, and when he did, he was very different from before. The burn about his ear had scarred, and his left arm was bound in a cast. His right leg, though now in one piece again, was encased in a metal shell of mechanical supports, shock absorbers, and splints. He walked with a heavy limp. His expression, which had once been friendly and open, was now dark, cold, and closed off.

Alexandria had given up on trying to approach other students altogether by that point. Nobody met her gaze in the halls, and she ignored them in turn. When Carter returned, he also created a notable distance between him and the other students, as they stayed out of his path. When he walked the halls, everyone backed away so far that the ends of his cape never even brushed their ankles. Funny, he thought, how after they had beaten and broken him, they now found him untouchable.

When lunch came, Alexandria found him at a lunch table in the far corner of the cafeteria.

"Hey," she said, sitting across from him. "Welcome back."

"Thanks," said Carter quietly. His eyes were downcast, and his right hand shook slightly as he ate.

"You okay?" Alexandria asked though she was pretty sure she knew the answer.

"No," he said. "I'm going to look like… like a freak, for the rest of my life. All because I got stuck going to a school that preaches vigilantism as a solution to everyone's problems."

"I know," Alexandria said, reaching over and putting a hand on his arm. "I can't believe how excited we used to be about this place."

Carter looked up to meet her gaze. "Have you been doing alright?"

"Fine," Alexandria said with a shrug. "Hopefully better with you back."

Carter smiled slightly. "Well, I'm glad to have you back, too," he said. "I hope they haven't gotten you into detention now that they're serving a life sentence in it."

"Nah, they've had to back off on that," Alexandria said with a smile.

"Good," said Carter. He sighed. "I would have pressed charges, but I figured that was more punishing their parents than punishing them. My dad's insurance paid for most of the medical bills, anyway." He cast a glare over at the empty table where the group used to sit. "They probably still think it was a good idea. Just beating up the villain, like any other hero." He rubbed his left arm ruefully. "I never thought I'd feel so bad for the villains. I guess I never thought people would think I was one."

"Yeah, me neither," Alexandria agreed.

"I don't think I'm cut out for being a hero," he said with a sigh.

"Yeah….I'm starting to wonder if that's even an option anymore," Alexandria said quietly. "For us, I mean."

Carter let his head fall to the table and he groaned. "I hate this school." The bell rang and the cafeteria began to clear. Carter stood slowly. "See you after school?"

"Definitely," Alexandria agreed.

Carter gave another small smile, then went to his class. Alexandria headed to her own class. It was interesting, she noted, how even though she wasn't the one ignoring the others, still no one met her gaze. She had decided several days before to adopt this method, she just walked like she belonged there- because she did. If everyone else wanted to avoid eye contact, they had to do it on purpose.

CHAPTER TWENTY-FIVE

During her next class, the other students were whispering together and casting glances her way, though careful to look away again if she turned to look at them. Alexandria waited a few moments, drumming her fingers on her desk.

"Do you have something to say to me?" she asked finally. The room fell dead silent. "Well, if you can't say it to my face, then shut up."

"So... how is Dr. Vile?" one kid asked.

"Who?" Alexandria asked, raising an eyebrow.

"Dr. Vile. It's Carter's supervillain name," said the guy. "You know, kind of like his face, with that scar on the side? Vile."

"Oh, that's very clever," Alexandria said sarcastically. "Have you got your own villain name worked out, too, then?"

"Um, I'm not a super-villain," said the guy with a confused frown.

"Oh, that's right," Alexandria said. "My bad, you have to have a certain level of intelligence for that, you wouldn't make the cut."

The guy scowled, and the room erupted into whispers again. Alexandria rolled her eyes and turned her attention to the class material. Nobody tried to speak to her again during class.

Another couple of weeks passed, and the group's detention was finished. It was barely two days later that Ed approached Alexandria once again in English.

"So, planning any new schemes?" said Ed.

Alexandria considered this a moment, then turned to face him, tossing her long blond hair over her shoulder.

"That's confidential," she said with a smile.

Ed blinked, then quickly went back to his seat, looking stunned and confused. Alexandria smirked and turned back to her work, satisfied. It seemed that he didn't know what to do next if she didn't get angry.

A few days later, Mori and a couple of his doubles approached Alexandria in the halls.

"I hear you're planning something," said Mori.

"Oh yes, quite extensive plans. They involve homework, mostly, and quality time with quality people," Alexandria said flatly. She kept walking and didn't slow. "That does not include you, by the way."

"I'm guessing you mean Dr. Vile, then," said Mori. "What, only back a few weeks later and he's already planning his next strike? You'd think he would take the time to recuperate in between schemes."

"Interesting you should say so," Alexandria said. "You seem to have recovered rather quickly from the fact that you and your friends scarred him for life for absolutely no reason. We're not scheming."

"Like you weren't scheming before," said Mori. "When you weren't scheming to mess up everyone's grades?"

"Oh, so you still think what you did was fair?" Alexandria said, rolling her eyes. "That's pretty pathetic, Mori, considering that 'scheme' was a prank with no lasting effects. You need to get yourself a better hobby."

"We stopped him before things got worse," said Mori. "That's what heroes do. They stop the bad guys."

"I've got news for you," Alexandria said, rounding on Mori. "You aren't heroes. You're just thugs." She glared down at him, she was about an inch taller, a few veins of pink energy crackled in her palms.

"And what, you think you're the hero?" said Mori. "If you don't know what you've turned into, then honestly, you're the only one who hasn't caught on yet."

Alexandria scowled, her eyes flashing the same color as her pink energy pulses.

"If you guys are the heroes, then I don't want to be on your side," Alexandria spat. She turned as if to leave, then suddenly swung at him, her fist aglow with pink energy so it never made contact as it sent Mori sprawling. "So leave me alone."

The Mori she hit disappeared, and the others glared at her.

"Villain," they said, then the rest disappeared, leaving her standing alone in the hall. Alexandria let out a frustrated breath, then turned to continue on her way to find Carter.

She found him waiting by his locker, as he always did, looking tired and in general irritated. When she came, he followed her out without a word, his mechanical leg brace creaking with every step. They walked most of the way home in silence, Alexandria trying to cool off a bit before talking to Carter, she still felt like she wanted to punch Mori again.

They set up to do homework in Carter's basement, and after a minute of staring at her paper and tapping her pencil, Alexandria said what was on her mind.

"So....are we just supposed to...to keep going like this?" Alexandria said, furrowing her brow. "I mean, trying not to stir up trouble, hoping we don't get caught in a dark alley or something?"

Carter looked at her with a deep, concerned frown. "They've been bothering you again?"

"Yeah," Alexandria said with a shrug, but she knew Carter wasn't fooled. "They just keep trying to get me to tell them your next evil scheme or whatever. That, and I think I might have almost gotten mugged by a couple of Mori after school, but they left after a few petty insults...."

Carter looked at her a long moment, trying to tell if she was alright, though he knew the answer. "I'm sorry," he said. "You don't have to live like this, you know. I'm the one they really hate; they're only after you because you stand up for me. If you wanted to, you could get them to accept you."

Alexandria looked up and gave him a small smile.

"Oh, I know that," Alexandria said. "But there's a reason I stand up for you, you know. It's because I'm not an idiot, not like them. I don't think I'd be any happier with friends like that, I wouldn't even have anyone good to fall back on. Not to mention, I would never trust them now."

Carter nodded, silent another moment. "Well... for the record, they're stupid to call you a villain. You're a hero to me."

"Thanks," Alexandria said, looking back down at the paper. "So don't go making any other stupid ideas for me to make friends with jerks. You're my best friend, Carter. That's not going to change."

Carter smiled. "Thanks."

Alexandria glanced over at Carter periodically as they worked. She tried not to think about anything else, that just made her angry. The worst part about it was that she didn't want to be thinking about these things, about not getting beat up, worrying about something happening to Carter, everything going on. There were a million other things she would rather think about. She wanted to think more about Carter, specifically, and she wanted him to think more about her; but not in a worried way. She wanted to think more about sitting close to each other, and holding hands, and laughing. She hated everything else for getting in the way.

Little did she know, however, that he was thinking about her. When she wasn't glancing at him, he glanced at her, and while he wasn't plotting any evil schemes… he was slowly developing a plan.

CHAPTER TWENTY-SIX

With the Christmas season came snow, and Carter braved the cold one night close to Christmas Break so sneak into the school, armed with a yuletide plan and decorations. He found locker number 384 and set to work, lacing it with tinsel and little gold and silver balls. With his power, he attached multi-colored strings of lights in a criss-cross pattern to the door, and finally, hanging from the top, he set a cluster of mistletoe trimmed into the shape of a heart. Satisfied with the result, he returned home, and the next day waited at lunch for the spectacular reaction it would no doubt create.

When Alexandria joined him at lunch, however, she mostly looked annoyed.

"Hey," she said, pulling out her lunch to eat. "I can't wait for the break."

"Oh, yeah," said Carter. "Are you alright?" Maybe she didn't like the decorations. Maybe she thought someone was making fun of her. He felt a knot form in his stomach.

"Yeah, I'm fine," Alexandria said with a shrug. "Just ready for a break from school drama. Gloria got some elaborate declaration of feelings from Mori this morning, the whole hall was celebrating." Alexandria rolled her eyes. "Her locker is next to mine, so that was a pain."

"Oh...," said Carter slowly. "So... Gloria's locker number is 384...?"

"Yeah, why?" Alexandria asked.

"Well, um..." Carter's face was white and he was having trouble forming words. How could he not know which locker was Alexandria's? I mean, sure she always met him at his locker, but he'd seen her use hers. Why'd he think hers was 384? "I... uh... may have made a mistake..."

Alexandria looked at him a moment, then realized what he was trying to say. She tried to stifle her amusement, then she started laughing and couldn't stop. Carter's face was bright red now, though he was struggling to maintain a straight face himself.

"So... what did you think of the decorations?" he said. Alexandria took a moment to compose herself, though still grinning widely.

"Well, with this new information," she said, "I think it's very sweet. Though….." she paused, drumming her fingers on the table thoughtfully.

"Oh, yeah, too much," said Carter, the sinking feeling returning, though his face remained frozen in a casual expression through his internal terror. "Sorry, maybe just a card or something next year, yeah?"

"No, no, that's not it," Alexandria said quickly, smiling. "I just thought mistletoe was….an odd choice if you weren't planning on seeing me until lunch…."

"Yeah, I guess that does seem silly," said Carter, trying very hard to stop flushing. "I just, you know, didn't want to make you feel pressured or anything. I mean, I didn't want to be one of those guys who just surprises somebody under mistletoe when you're, you know, not actually dating or have any prior consent."

Alexandria laughed and reached over and took his hand. "That's very sweet of you."

Carter smiled. "Well, I mean, I have some more in my backpack if, you know, that's something that you want to do right now. No pressure or anything, I mean, the locker one was supposed to be kind of a suggestion, not like you have to." He stopped, realizing he was rambling.

"I don't know…," Alexandria said. "The cafeteria wasn't exactly the setting I envisioned this happening in…."

"Oh, right," said Carter. His brain felt like it was covered with a blank piece of paper. "Um, do you want to go somewhere else…? Or, you know, maybe another time. Sorry, I didn't really think this through as well as I'd thought."

Alexandria laughed again, but he could tell the moment was gone.

"Yeah, I don't think this is the time…" Alexandria said, trying to mask the awkwardness that had filled the situation.

"Yeah…" said Carter. "Well… Merry Christmas." Alexandria snorted, then put a hand to her face.

"Sorry, sorry," she said, smiling. "That was just…funny."

Carter grinned. "Hey, I'll take funny." He dug into his lunch, giving her an extra cookie that he always packed. It had become a tradition now, one of his favorite traditions.

Not soon enough, school was out for the year in anticipation of Christmas. The first few days of Christmas break, Carter didn't hear anything from Alexandria as her parents had decided to take an impromptu skiing trip with some of their extended family. They kept in contact, however, through text, and when her family pulled up in the driveway of their house, he was waiting by their front door. Just like Gloria's locker door, her front door was now decorated with tinsel, lights, and Christmas orbs, and a cluster of mistletoe hung from the doorframe.

"Hey," he said jokingly as she stepped out of the car. "This is the right door this time, yeah?"

"If you got my house wrong, I'd punch you," Alexandria said with a laugh, quickly climbing out and running over to him, nearly slipping on the ice in the process. There was now a defined tan-line around her eyes from her ski goggles. He caught her as she came up the stairs, one hand on the railing to keep himself steady and his other hand catching hers to help her up.

Alexandria's parents seemed to be taking an extraordinarily long amount of time to get out of the car. Alexandria turned her head so she was looking at him out of the corner of her eye.

"So," she said, "Are you going to kiss me or not?"

Carter felt a buzz of excitement in the back of his head, then kissed her, once on the mouth. "Merry Christmas," he said.

"Merry Christmas," Alexandria said, wrapping him in a hug.

Then, the front door opened suddenly, to reveal Alexandria's parents. Her mom had a camera in hand and her dad was grinning maniacally. Somehow they had snuck in the back.

"Alright, get in here, lovebirds," her dad said, pulling them inside.

Carter flushed, coming inside as directed, though still holding Alexandria's hand. Mrs. Luxe ushered them inside, sitting Carter down on the couch and then taking Alexandria into the kitchen 'to make hot chocolate,' leaving Carter in the living room with Mr. Luxe, who proceeded to stare Carter down in silence for several long seconds.

"So…" said Carter, "how was the ski trip?"

"Good," Mr. Luxe said, he crossed his arms, clearly employing a great deal of effort to keep a straight face. "So, you should know, if you're going to start dating Alexandria, there are some rules."

"Alright," said Carter.

At that point, Mr. Luxe finally lost his composure and laughed, resting his hands on his knees as he doubled over.. "Fortunately, I'm pretty sure the only way you'd even think of breaking them," he said, "is if I told you what they were."

Carter relaxed. "Is one of them 'no PDA in the doorway'?" he joked.

"Nope, you're safe," Mr. Luxe said. He clapped Carter on the shoulder. "You're a good kid, I think you'll know if you're about to do something you shouldn't."

"Thanks," said Carter.

"And even if you didn't," Mr. Luxe said with a wink, "Alexandria would, and we both know she's got a good right hook."

Carter chuckled. "It's true," he said. "I've seen it."

"Great, well, if that's settled," Mr. Luxe said, getting up, "Let's go see how the hot chocolate is coming. You sticking around for a while?"

"If that's alright," said Carter. "I can drive myself home, though."

"Well, you're always welcome here," Mr. Luxe said with a nod, heading into the kitchen.

"Thanks," said Carter, and he followed Mr. Luxe into where Alexandria and her mom were making the hot chocolate.

The two families decided to have Christmas day together, and they set up the presents for both at the Luxe's. Carter and Mr. Greys showed up early in the most ridiculous Christmas sweaters they could find, and bearing a tray of Christmas cookies and candy canes.

Alexandria opened the door, wearing red and white striped Christmas pajamas, to let them in. Christmas music blasted through the house on full volume. They put the tray of cookies with the other Christmas treats, including eggnog and cinnamon rolls with an assortment of fruit, in the middle of the living room where the tree and presents were. Carter and Alexandria sat on the floor and passed out the presents while the adults talked on the couches.

Carter pulled out a present wrapped in green Christmas tree wrapping paper and tied with a red bow and passed it to Alexandria.

"That one is from me," he said.

"Ooh, what could it be?" Alexandria said with a smile, briefly examining the gift to try and guess. She wasn't that determined to guess, however and quickly tore off the paper. Out of the box spilled a sparkling pink cape made of a silky material, wrapped around a book Alexandria had been dying to read: The Witch's Mask.

Alexandria laughed and leaned over and hugged him.

"You're the best."

Carter hugged her back.

"What, you thought I was going to leave you out of all the cape-wearing fun this Christmas?" he asked. He reached into his backpack by the couch and pulled out his own cape. "Now we can celebrate in style."

"Perfect," Alexandria said, putting on her new cape. "Well, don't be disappointed by your gift, it's not nearly as great as this."

"That's alright," he said, searching the tree for his gift. "Nothing is as great as that cape."

He found his gift, a small package wrapped in blue snowflake paper, tucked under the tree. Inside was a journal with a double sided pen, one regular side and one with invisible ink. Carter grinned.

"That's awesome," he said. Then he laughed. "Now I can write down all of my 'evil schemes' without the rest of the student body finding them."

"Exactly," Alexandria said with a sly gleam in her eye.

"You're amazing," said Carter. He leaned over and gave her a kiss on the cheek. Mr. Greys clapped and threw confetti made of ripped up wrapping paper on them.

CHAPTER TWENTY-SEVEN

The break ended, and Carter, having fully embraced his "evil" identity at this point, kept the bullies away by leaving scraps of paper with invisible ink messages lying around to keep them too busy to harass him. After a few days being back, and again being pestered incessantly about Carter's activities, Alexandria wore her own new cape to school, also wearing a smile that dared anyone to challenge her.

Of course, neither method was perfectly effective, but it made school bearable and took some of the edge off of the hisses of "villain" and dirty looks that followed them in the halls. Then, as February rolled in, people started to become more distracted by their girlfriends and boyfriends than in trying to make Carter and Alexandria miserable. With the lax in "hero" activity, Carter decided it was once again time for another 'scheme.'

It was the end of class just as the bell for lunch rang on Valentine's day, and all of the power in the school went out with a faint electric pop. People pulled out their phones to use as flashlights, and teachers went to look for electric lanterns in the utility closets. Alexandria stepped into the hall to go to lunch, then stopped at the sight of a path made by rows of rose-colored Christmas lights on the floor, leading up to the doorway of her classroom. Only the ones closest to the door were lit, and as she stepped into the hall, the ones behind her blinked out and more lit up in front of her.

Alexandria smiled and followed the lights. The bulbs continued to light up just a few steps ahead of her as she walked, keeping in perfect sync with her steps. It lead her down the halls and to the cafeteria, then to the table where she and Carter always sat, though it had been moved out of the corner and into the center of the room. The lights came to make a ring around the table, and the table itself was set with a homemade lunch lit by fake candlelight, and Carter stood beside it all holding a bouquet of roses.

"I'm impressed," Alexandria said when she made it to him. "You're quite the mastermind."

"Yeah, well, I've been planning this particular scheme for a while," he said, smiling. "So... will you be my valentine?"

"Of course," Alexandria said with a smile, then hugged him. "Hopefully our fan club doesn't make a scene, though."

Carter held her tight. "Ah, I wouldn't worry about that," he said. "I may have mentioned to Mori that the truth of who decorated Gloria's locker could get out should he or the others get involved in this instance. This is the only time he's going to let me pull that card, of course, but... I think it's worth it."

Alexandria smiled and leaned her head on his shoulder. "I think so, too."

They stood together a moment longer, holding each other before Carter kissed Alexandria on the top of the head and they went to sit and eat. The food was as well planned as the rest of the display, consisting of hard boiled eggs dyed pink, sandwiches with red jelly filling cut into heart shapes, and pink heart-shaped cookies with glittery sprinkles, reminiscent of Alexandria's cape.

The other students kept their distances, sending only glances and whispers their way. One phrase made it clearly to Carter and Alexandria's ears: "Dr. Vile and his Valentine."

"Hm," Alexandria said thoughtfully, "You know, I think that's a nickname I can live with."

"Well, I certainly can't complain," said Carter, smiling. "Though my reasons are a bit selfish."

"I wouldn't worry about that," Alexandria said with a grin. "They're all jealous anyway."

"Maybe they should try a bit harder to show appreciation to their girlfriends, then," said Carter. He reached into his backpack and pulled out a bottle of carbonated cranberry juice, opening it with a pop. He filled two champagne glasses and set them on the table with the rest.

"They should take notes," Alexandria agreed. She knew the other students, the self-proclaimed heroes, would probably use this against them somehow later, but she couldn't bring herself to care at the moment. They clinked glasses, and toasted to "Dr. Vile and his Valentine."

CHAPTER TWENTY-EIGHT

Another month passed without any serious incident. The students continued to whisper and glance, keeping their distances. The yearbook committee were the only ones who got closer than the occasional hallway jeer, following them around for pictures to put on their "villain page" in the yearbook. Carter and Alexandria settled into the habit of ignoring them all for the most part, and everything settled into a semblance of normalcy.

Carter and Alexandria went back and forth between studying at one another's homes. They were at Alexandria's, eyes plastered to textbook pages when the doorbell rang.

"Want me to get it?" said Carter. At this point, any excuse to drop the textbook would be welcome.

"Sure," Alexandria said. "It's probably our neighbor looking for her cat, just tell her we haven't seen it."

Carter nodded and limped down the stairs. His leg had healed for the most part, though there was extensive nerve and tendon damage that the doctors said would likely never heal, leaving him with permanent weakness in that leg. He was still working to improve the brace he'd made to compensate, though it still squeaked a bit when he walked and wasn't quite as flexible as he'd like.

He answered the door and found two police officers standing with solemn faces. Carter hesitated.

"Is Alexandria Luxe at home?" said one of the officers before Carter could speak.

Carter nodded. "Um, is something wrong?"

The officers didn't answer. Carter turned his head to call up the stairs. "Uh, Alexandria? The police are here, they say they want to speak to you..."

"Um, okay, I'm coming," Alexandria's voice called back, sounding bewildered, and also a bit apprehensive. She came down the stairs somewhat cautiously. "Can I help you, officers?"

"I'm sorry, Miss Luxe," said the officer. "There's... been an incident at the bank. Your parents were caught in a hostage situation and.... they didn't make it out."

Alexandria stopped short, staring at them, her face quickly draining of color.

"I...um....are you sure?" she asked quietly after a moment. Carter moved to her side and put his arm around her shoulders to steady her.

"Yes, I'm sorry," said the officer. "We're going to need to take you with us while social services contact your relatives-,"

"Hey, no way," said Carter. "She can stay with my family, she's not going to stay in a police station."

Alexandria didn't move, still staring at the officers. She didn't seem to notice the ongoing conversation between them and Carter.

"Where are they?" she asked, her voice trembling. The officers shifted uncomfortably, not wanting to respond.

"We'll need to verify with your parents and have them sign some papers if she's going to stay with them," said the other officer to Carter. Carter recited his home number and address to them, not daring to let go of Alexandria to write it down himself.

"Where are they?" Alexandria repeated, more forcefully as she blinked her eyes back into focus. Tears spilled out onto her cheeks. "I need to see them."

"They're at the station morgue," said the officer. "I'm sorry, Miss. Once we contact your extended family, we can have them moved to the funeral home of their choice." He looked at Carter. "We'll contact your parents. Would you like us to give you a ride there?"

"No, no I think I'll have my dad come here," said Carter. He looked at Alexandria. "Do you want to go sit down?"

Alexandria nodded, looking away from the officers. The implications were slowly crashing down on her, she wasn't sure she quite believed them yet. Her parents couldn't be gone, they couldn't be dead. It didn't make any sense. Thinking about it, it felt like there was a hole being torn open inside of her.

Carter moved her to the couch. The officers didn't leave, but rather lingered in the house, not daring to leave them alone with the news. Carter himself felt sick, stunned, and oddly cold and empty. He felt like he should be falling apart, like Alexandria. Her parents had been like family to him, too, after all, but he just felt... nothing, like some part of him was on autopilot. His mind was working it like a puzzle. He had to stay with Alexandria, hold her while she cried, make her something warm to drink. He had to make sure she had a place to stay, that she was supported, that she wasn't traumatized any more than she already was. It was like he didn't even have emotions, no opinion on the matter at all. There was only the next step, the task at hand, the girlfriend to comfort.

The officers called Mr. Greys while Carter held Alexandria on the couch. Once Alexandria started really crying, she dissolved into uncontrollable sobbing. Carter didn't speak a word.

Mr. Greys arrived and spoke to the officers a while. Then he helped Alexandria into his car with Carter and drove them home, leaving the cops behind. He set up the guest room and made them all cider to drink before joining Carter in comforting Alexandria.

"It'll be alright, you'll be alright," he kept saying, keeping a comforting hand on Alexandria's shoulder. His eyes welled with tears as he spoke, though he didn't fall apart. He just kept repeating the words, over and over, trying to make them true.

"Thank you," Alexandria said eventually. "I think....I need some sleep....can you just let me know if they call? The police, about anything?"

Mr. Greys nodded, and he pulled Carter away. It was hard, Carter stiffened at his touch and at first refused to move from her side, until Mr. Greys spoke sharply for him to let her rest, and he marched Carter out. Carter's hands began to shake once they closed the door behind them.

"We... we shouldn't leave her alone, not right now," Carter mumbled.

"She'll be alright, she just needs some rest," said Mr. Greys. Carter didn't register, finally starting to cry. Mr. Greys pulled him away, down the hall to the sitting room, where he held Carter and both wept.

Alexandria stayed with the Greys through the funeral that was held two days later. She didn't return to school with Carter after the weekend, however, instead electing to stay home and take time to recover. Carter knew she still spent a lot of time crying when she was alone.

At school wasn't much better; all anyone could talk about was the heroes and their daring rescue of twenty of the twenty-three civilians in the bank. Emilia and Gloria especially received a lot of praise and attention; their parents were the ones who had made the rescue. Thankfully, at least while Alexandria was gone from school, Dr. Vile and his Valentine were an almost forgotten topic. Almost.

When Alexandria returned, she was approached by one of Emilia's hangers-on, a girl named Charlotte.

"Hey, Principal wants to see you after classes," she said. Alexandria sighed and looked over at her. She wasn't feeling up to giving her sarcastic comebacks yet.

"Why?" she asked.

"Dunno," said Charlotte with a shrug. "Probably to transfer you to another school or something."

Alexandria groaned and turned away. "I don't know why I ask you anything."

"I've been wondering something, though," said Charlotte. "Out of all of those civilians, your parents are the ones that get killed. Do you think the heroes did it on purpose? Like they knew you were a villain?"

Alexandria didn't say anything for a moment, blinking back tears. Then she looked over at Charlotte.

"What...is the matter with you?" Alexandria asked, her tone soft but angry, barely controlled. "What have I ever done to you? You have a sick, twisted mind."

"Hey, chill, it was just a thought. It just seemed rather convenient is all," said Charlotte defensively. She walked quickly off, casting an irritated look back at Alexandria. Alexandria glared at her, then looked away. Tears were streaming down her face. It was a horrible thought, but she couldn't help wonder if Charlotte was right about the heroes.

A minute or two later, Carter came walking her way down the hall. He didn't stop or speak, but just walked right up and pulled her into a hug.

"Are you alright?" he asked quietly, still holding her.

"No," Alexandria whispered, leaning into him and crying harder. She couldn't even pretend to be alright anymore.

"We're skipping first period," said Carter, "Let's get some fresh air."

CHAPTER TWENTY-NINE

They sat on the bleachers on the far side of the football field in silence. Alexandria had cried herself dry and now just stared down at the dirt, hugging her backpack in front of her.

"What did they say?" said Carter. "I know it was something cruel, that's what they always do."

"It was….she thinks…." Alexandria said, then took a breath to try and steady herself. "The heroes….they might have let my parents die." Her voice shook and she closed her eyes. "Because of me. Because I'm….because I'm a villain."

Carter put an arm around her shoulders, using his free hand to hold hers. "They're idiots," he said.

"But what if it's true?" Alexandria said, her voice catching. "What if…."

Carter looked down, feeling sick to his stomach. "I… I don't know." He sighed. "I mean, a year ago I would have said it was ridiculous, but…"

"Me too," Alexandria said quietly. "But now…"

"They sure raised some twisted kids, I'll say that much," said Carter bitterly. "Who knows, I mean, that might have been where they learned it."

"Maybe that's what all of them are like," Alexandria said. She hated it, and them. She hated all of them, for everything they had done to Carter, and to her, and maybe even her parents.

"They keep calling us villains," said Carter. "I'm starting to wonder… maybe we should be. I mean, if those are the heroes, well, I don't think I want to be on their side anymore."

Alexandria was silent for several minutes. She didn't want to just prove them right, but she wanted them to pay for everything they had done. She knew she couldn't keep going on like this, it was all too much. They were never going to let her get anywhere if she kept trying to play by their rules.

"I think....you might be right," she said finally.

"I mean, if I hear one more person congratulating Emilia for what her mom did, I'm going to be sick," said Carter angrily. "They have no right to treat you like this, not before, and especially not now."

"There's nothing we can do to change their minds anyway," Alexandria said, bitterness creeping into her voice. "They'll think we're villains no matter what we do, no matter how hard we try. Not striking back....it just makes it easier for them to hurt us."

"Exactly," said Carter. "And, I mean, there's not much they can do to punish us at this point anyway, not anything they haven't already done or are already doing." He took a deep breath, then looked at her. "So... I was thinking, want to wreck this school with me?"

Alexandria nodded.

"Yeah....yeah, definitely," she said.

Carter gave a grim smile and squeezed her hand in his.

Later that day, they ran from the school, followed by fire alarms, small, popping explosions, an insane amount of smoke, no less than eight angry teachers, and the principal. Carter was wearing a mechanical suit built entirely from the computers and other electronic contents of the computer lab, and Alexandria's eyes and fingers were still glowing and sparking with pink energy. Both were filled with a rush of adrenaline, and Carter scooped Alexandria up in his arms and took off flying out of the city and into the mountains, disappearing from the grasp of the school staff.

Alexandria laughed as they flew off, her arms wrapped around Carter's neck.

"I definitely feel better," she called over the wind.

Carter grinned. "Me too."

They landed on a mountain overlook, with thick clusters of evergreens behind them and the whole valley before them. Carter set her down and sat down, letting some of the mechanical suit fall away.

"Did you see their faces?" he said. "I thought Emilia was going to melt her desk."

Alexandria smiled, sprawling out on the ground and letting the grass lace through her fingers.

"It was great," Alexandria said. "They are never going to forget this day."

"Yeah," said Carter. His smile faltered a bit. "We probably won't be able to go back there again. Not for school, anyway, and... I dunno, I don't want to make my dad harbor fugitives. The police will be after us for that, you know."

"Yeah...for sure," Alexandria said, staring up at the sky thoughtfully. "I don't want to do that to your dad either, we'll need somewhere else to stay. Got any ideas?"

"Well..." Carter looked around at the mountainside. "This place has a nice view. What do you think? I build a giant robot, we set up some walls and rob an IKEA, this place could turn out pretty nice."

Alexandria sat up and looked around, then smiled and laughed.

"That sounds great," she said. "It sounds perfect."

Carter grinned, then rearranged the mechanical components he'd pulled into his mech suit and formed a hover platform instead. He stepped up and put a hand out for Alexandria to join him. She took his hand, and they took off together towards Mr. Grey's house.

When they arrived, Carter's father was standing on the lawn, arms folded.

"The school called me," he said. "What do you two have to say for yourselves?"

Alexandria glanced at Carter, holding his hand tightly, then back at Mr. Greys.

"Well...we're not sorry," Alexandria said.

"I'm just here to pick up some things," said Carter, a bit more fiercely than he'd intended. "Then we're leaving." He looked away. "You won't have to worry about us messing things up for you."

Mr. Greys shook his head and looked at them with sad, heartbroken eyes.

"I only want to help you, Carter," he said. "You're my son, you can't mess anything up for me."

"Well... we can't stay," said Carter, his voice shaking. "We tried to make it work, Dad, but we can't. And we can't stay. The police will come and then it'll be over. We have to go."

Tears welled in his eyes, and Mr. Greys came forward and hugged them both tightly. "Well, if you're running away, let's make sure you're not going empty-handed," he said.

Alexandria closed her eyes as she hugged him back.

"Thank you, Mr. Greys," she said.

"Think nothing of it," he said. "You stood by my son, didn't you?" He pulled away. "Come inside, you should have time to pack before anyone comes looking for you here."

They followed Mr. Greys inside and packed while he prepared lunch for them. While they packed and ate, he took their measurements and scribbled down the results on his sketchpad.

"What are you doing?" said Carter. "I mean... we won't need hero suits, you know we're not going to be heroes."

"You think I've only ever made a suit for heroes?" said Mr. Greys with a slight smile. "I'm flattered by your high opinion of me, but I've done plenty for supervillains as well. From what I hear of your escapades, that's what you're looking to be, isn't it?"

"Well, yeah, I guess so," Alexandria said. She was still getting used to the idea. "It seems like our best option."

"Then I want to make sure you're at least dressed properly," said Mr. Greys. "I can't stop you, but I can prepare you as best I can, and I carry the philosophy that everyone, hero or villain, deserves to have something to wear that was made by someone who cares for their safety."

Alexandria smiled. "You're the best."

"Thank you," said Mr. Greys with a returned smile. He sat down and started sketching. "Though I do wonder... are you sure you want to become villains? I mean, it's a hard life, or so I hear."

"It can't be worse than what we've already been through," said Carter. "We're already living as villains, and we didn't even do anything wrong. We've been model students and model citizens our whole lives, and look where that's gotten us." He looked down at his plate. "Besides... if they're going to be the future heroes, then we'll never be left alone, no matter what we do. We'll always be villains to them."

"Carter's right," Alexandria said. "Honestly, the least we can do is make it hard for them to make us miserable. And, at least this way, we can make them pay for what they've done. They don't get to just....go on and never think about it."

Mr. Greys nodded, saddened but having no argument left. "Alright," he said. "A villain's suit it is, then. You two can start getting your things ready to go, I'll get to work on your clothes in the basement."

"Thanks," Alexandria said. Her stuff was, fortunately, mostly packed already. Once she finished eating, she put away what was scattered through the house, stuffing it in her bags. Carter did the same, then ran out to the garage to pull all of his materials there into a great hover vehicle that would hold both their belongings and his tech.

The police came by to take statements. Mr. Greys played the part of a confused and grieving father while Alexandria and Carter hid. They stayed the night after that while Mr. Greys worked on their suits, using technology that Carter had helped him build to speed up the process. The next morning, close to lunch, Mr. Greys showed them their new clothes.

Alexandria's had a base color of sky blue, accented with varying shades of pink to resemble her energy powers. A magenta cape hung from the shoulders down to her ankles, made of a shimmery material. A pair of knee-high boots of the same color scheme completed the outfit.

Mr. Greys handed her a bottle of some kind of leave-in hair conditioner.

"This will help keep your hair repelled by your energy, so you don't singe it," he said, "and I think you'll like the effect of the way your hair will move when you use your powers, like being blown by an electric wind."

"It's great, thanks," Alexandria said with a smile. She tucked the bottle into her bag.

Mr. Greys smiled sadly. "You've always had very nice hair, don't let anyone tell you otherwise," he said. "I'd hate to see you damage it in your new line of work. Take care of the rest of you, too, alright?"

"I will," Alexandria said.

Carter's suit was mostly mechanical, and Carter knew just by looking at it that he'd be making some improvements for efficiency. The cloth underneath, however, was very light and soft, and the suit carried its own temperature control. It was all black with lines of electric green, and his helmet split down the middle in front of his face, able to fold away to only cover the top of his head and the sides to reveal his face while still covering the scar by his ear. The cape was long and lined with a special material that could catch and absorb energy, fire, and plasma attacks, and the collar, of course, was high and pointed at the front, with a hidden button along the top corner to close it against the wind. Carter smiled.

"Thanks, Dad," he said. Mr. Greys nodded, eyes watering. He couldn't help himself and pulled Carter into a hug.

"Don't keep that mask on too much, I want people to see my son's handsome face," he said. Carter hugged him back, tightly.

"Thanks," Carter said again, blinking away his own tears. Finally, they pulled apart.

"Be careful," said Mr. Greys, wiping his eyes. "And if you need me, please, always come home. I don't care what trouble you bring with you, it wouldn't possibly compare to the threat of losing you."

Carter nodded, wiping his own eyes as well. Then he stepped back and took Alexandria's hand.

"Let's go."

Alexandria nodded, giving his hand a squeeze. They put their things in the hover vehicle, stepped in together, then took off back towards the mountains.

CHAPTER THIRTY

The lair only took a few days to build. Carter used his machines to quickly and effectively build up the house itself, stealing whatever materials they needed with ease. He built a cloaking device to shield the house from sight and physical attacks, and also built a giant robot because he reasoned, every supervillain should have one. It was much better than a forklift, anyway.

The cloaking device covered their house and the surrounding area that they designated to be their yard, which was immense. The house was large and luxurious in design, and Carter took much time and care in picking out the paint colors for the walls. The interior was decorated with entire sections stolen from IKEA, courtesy of the giant robot. After much deliberation, they decided the robot had to stay out of the yard and gave it its own cave and cloaking device beneath the house on the side of a cliff.

For a time, more than a month, Alexandria immensely enjoyed just being away from everything, alone up in the mountains. She helped design the house, and then did most of the decorating herself, rearranging things quite a bit until she was satisfied.

Eventually, though, her enjoyment of solitude ran down so she welcomed the opportunity to get out and do something. That was how she ended up at the store that day, picking up food.

She wore a casual, nondescript outfit with a hat and sunglasses. She avoided the pink and blue combination that would clue people into her identity, as she and Carter had already gained some notoriety. The store was busy with shoppers and some just looking to escape the summer heat.

When Alexandria was at the checkout, her card was rejected. The flustered cashier tried to fix it, and then the screen flashed red.

Glancing around, Alexandria noticed guns being pulled from concealed locations in purses and hidden holsters. Undercover police started to surround her, though they were wary.

"Put your hands in the air, step away from the cashier," one of the police said firmly. "You're under arrest!"

Alexandria looked at him, then dove to the side, landing behind a checkout counter for cover. Several bullets whizzed past her, just barely missing. Alexandria's heart raced as she quickly scanned the area.

Her hands pulsed with pink energy. She was glad that she was at least wearing body armor under her clothes. Alexandria took a deep breath, then sprang from her position. She shot bolts of energy and the cops nearest her and ran towards the nearest exit. She winced as the bullets she didn't dodge made painful impact.

Alexandria jumped into the air, her feet becoming encased in the energy so that when she landed, there was virtually no friction between her and the floor, and she shot past the officers and out the door.

Once outside, she was encased in a bubble of water, controlled by a caped man in a blue colored jumpsuit. Alexandria held her breath, then shot a bolt of energy at the man, forcefully enough to break out of the water. She had to get out before she ran out of air. The man dodged easily, and then, out of the corner of her eye, she saw Emilia's mother approach, dressed in blinding yellow and orange and hands crackling with electricity.

Alexandria's heart raced, and she sent a volley of energy bolts out at them in rapid succession. It was taking a lot of her energy, but she didn't have another choice. Her bolts were deflected as another member of the league came into view, casting forcefields to protect the other members. Emilia's mother circled around behind Alexandria.

"Nice try, kid," was the last thing Alexandria heard from her before she stuck her hands into the water and electricity coursed through her body. Alexandria involuntary inhaled a lungful of water, then slipped away into unconsciousness.

CHAPTER THIRTY-ONE

When she woke, she was in a high-security prison cell, blocked off by an electric field instead of bars. Alexandria scowled, then held out her hand and shot a blast of energy at the field. The electric field absorbed the blast with a quiet crackle, but overall there was no effect. The floor and ceiling both deflected her attacks when she tried them, sending energy bouncing around the room until it hit the field and disappeared.

Alexandria gave up that approach, then lay back on the hard bed with a sigh. Carter would break her out, she was confident of that. She just wondered how long it would take.

A few hours later, a man in a formal suit and sunglasses came to stand in front of her cell.

"Aren't you rather young to be a super-villain?" he said.

Alexandria turned to look at him, propping her head up on her hand.

"Am I?" she asked.

"Very," said the man. "It's a pity; you and your friend are throwing away a bright future with your actions."

"Hm, well, see the hero quota had been filled up for our year," Alexandria said. "But we weren't quite ready to give up, so we took the next best option."

"There may still be an opening for you," said the man. "Come on, Alexandria, don't let a few mistakes ruin your chance at a good life. Tell us where your friend is, let us help you get your lives back on track."

"And who are you, exactly?" Alexandria asked.

"My name is Agent Peter Matthews, but you can call me Pete," said the man with a friendly smile.

"Hm, I don't think we're quite on a first name basis," Alexandria said. "I'm guessing you work with a lot of heroes. Like the ones that put me here."

"I do," said Pete. "I also work with a lot of kids like you, kids who've gotten themselves into a bit of trouble with the law."

Alexandria sat up and looked at him with mock sincerity.

"Oh, and I am sure you just have my best interests at heart, you know there's good in everyone, and every cloud has a silver lining," she said with an exaggerated nod. Then she smirked, amused. "I don't buy it, Agent Matthews. I've met a few too many heroes at this point. You just want me to rat out my friend so you can lock us both up. Well, it's not happening."

"I want you to tell me where your friend is so I can help both of you," said Pete. "You don't have to live like this. Your friend can go home to his father, you can both go home. But I can't help you if you don't give me something to work with, Alexandria. You've got to show me that you want to change, that you want your life back, and then I can help you get it. That's how this works."

"No, that's not how this works," Alexandria said coldly. "And it's thanks to your heroes that I don't even have a home to go to. That's all on them. And you know what? I'm done with them, done playing their game and playing nice. I tried that, and it just didn't work. This is what works."

"But it's not working, is it," said the man. "Otherwise you wouldn't be here, and your friend wouldn't be out there all by himself. Please, Alexandria, work with me. If not for your sake, for Carter's. Trust me, you want me to find him before the heroes do. You don't want him to get hurt. Help me find him, and then we can stop this nightmare."

"Found him," said Carter, coming around the corner of the hall just a few yards away. He was dressed in his mechanical villain suit, with the cover over his face. With the suit on, his limp was barely even noticeable, and he looked taller, more powerful.

Pete pulled a gun out and turned to fire at Carter, but Carter brought him down with a flash of lightning.

"There you are," Alexandria said with a smile, standing. "I was wondering when you'd show up. They were going to bring out bad cop soon, that could have gotten tedious."

"You know I'd never let it get that far," said Carter, and though she couldn't see his face, she could tell he was grinning. He walked over to the cell and deactivated the field from the outside. His mask folded away and he gave her a concerned look. "Are you alright?"

"I'm fine, better now that you're here," Alexandria said. "How long have I been gone?"

"Less than a day," said Carter. "The whole thing was a trap from what I could find out. I think someone recognized you last time you went shopping and they set up the whole thing." He smiled slightly. "I think we've got them scared."

"Maybe they should be," Alexandria said. She took his hand and looked around. "Let's get out of here. I'm ready for some sleep in my own bed, theirs sucks."

Carter snorted, then took her hand, pulling her to stand beside him. With his free hand, he pressed a button on his arm, and after a pause, the ceiling was peeled away by a large, metal hand. Together, they stepped up onto the next metal hand that came down in front of them, and they were lifted out of the prison walls and high above the building. Alarms rang and lights flashed beneath them, but Carter silenced it all with one last blast of electricity. Locks clicked open, and inmates started running out of the building in waves.

"Prison break!" Carter yelled, raising a fist, and the inmates cheered in response. Some of them began to fly away while others blasted down the remaining barriers with various powers, and agents were running everywhere in a futile attempt to regain control.

"I think that should keep them busy," Alexandria said with a grin.

"Oh yes," said Carter, looking down with pride at the chaos they'd created. "Let's leave them to their work and head home, shall we?"

Alexandria nodded.

"We shall."

CHAPTER THIRTY-TWO

They spent the next two or so years pulling fantastical heists, mostly harmless. First, instead of painting the town red, they painted the town pink. Every building, with the help of an army of robots in the middle of the night, was painted a blinding shade of hot pink. They also robbed a convenience store and TP'd the city hall, set all of the healthy animal shelter animals free in office buildings all over the city, and in the winter, they rigged machines all over the city that would shoot unsuspecting passersby with snowballs.

The public, particularly reporters, were soon all over it. They quickly figured out that Dr. Vile and Valentine were not a threat to them if they happened upon a heist in the works, so long as they didn't bring weapons or heroes. Because of this, their names were taking up more headlines than anything else whenever they pulled a heist, big or small. Alexandria loved playing into it when the reporters were there. Sometimes they would use their heists to promote causes, like hacking news stations to air self-made commercials to encourage donations to charities, like one that gave shoes to foster kids, or for people facing natural disasters. Once they even froze up the local stock exchange until every big company had donated 10,000 dollars to local charities and small businesses.

Of course, they saved a fair number of heists for themselves as well, allowing them to gather materials and set up overseas funds, working with other villains to set up a network of people ready to back them up should any of them get arrested. Carter created a virus that would hack into the wealthier, more corrupt corporations and send money to him and his allies.

Over time, their hideout in the mountains evolved, becoming more of what they wanted and less of what they didn't use. As Alexandria liked to describe it, it was becoming more "elegant." Carter, through some of his connections, was also able to buy off the land they were on as private property under a false name, allowing them to put up a small road leading up to the hideout, as well as a fence and many "keep out" signs to avoid anyone awkwardly wandering into their cloaking field.

Carter had his robotic assistants clean up the house one day, sending Alexandria to pick up some groceries while they worked. Alexandria's secret identity look had gotten more refined over the past few years, and with the help of a smaller version of Carter's cloaking device, she didn't really have to worry about being recognized anymore.

When she returned and came out of the car, pink and red rose petals fell from the sky around her, dropped by a currently invisible giant robot.

Alexandria smiled and headed inside.

"Alright, what's up, Carter?" Alexandria asked, looking around. Carter was nowhere in sight, but a path of stemless roses and rose petals led the way to the backyard. Alexandria laughed slightly, she had always liked his flair for the dramatic, and followed the trail.

Outside, Carter stood barefoot next to a large picnic blanket, set with strawberry lemonade and two plates of spaghetti. The entire yard between them was covered in stemless roses and petals. He quickly walked to her side and, before she could say anything, slipped her shoes off her feet and took her hand.

"Join me for dinner?" he said with a smile.

"Oh, I suppose," Alexandria said. The roses were soft and velvety under her feet as they walked over to the picnic. Carter had timed everything perfectly so the sun was just setting over the horizon when they sat down to eat, cooling the air and the flower petals. Alexandria sighed deeply, leaning her head on Carter's shoulder.

"This is nice," she said.

"I'm glad you like it," he said. He shifted the plates so they could comfortably reach them, and they ate and talked at their leisure as the night came on and the first stars began to come out. Just as it was becoming dark, rose-colored lights came on around them, bathing them and the flowers in a soft glow.

"You always think of everything," Alexandria said. "If you're not careful, you won't be able to outdo yourself the next time."

"Well, I was hoping tonight would be unforgettable," said Carter. He pulled away, then dropped to one knee in front of her and pulled out a ring from his pocket. It was a thick, gold band, decorated with rubies of varying shades to form what looked like tiny, glittering roses.

"Alexandria, my Valentine," said Carter, "will you marry me?"

Alexandria laughed, tackling him in a hug so they both fell over. She had closed her hand around his and the ring.

"You know what? I want this to make headlines," Alexandria said with a grin.

"Oh, a public wedding, is it?" said Carter, exaggeratedly serious. "We could abduct a priest."

"As public as possible," Alexandria said. "We'll have to kidnap my reporter friends, too."

"Of course, of course, and my father," said Carter. "Though I don't think he'll mind quite as much as the priest will."

"He would mind a lot more if he wasn't invited," Alexandria said. "Oh, and I'm going to need to go dress shopping."

"Sounds like a good opportunity for a crime spree," said Carter. "I can keep the heroes busy while you hold up some dress shops."

"Sounds perfect," Alexandria said. She smiled, everything did seem perfect.

"In the meantime..." Carter said with a smile. Soft violin music began to play from the speakers hidden in the porch nearby. "Would you like to share a dance with me in the flowers?"

"I would love to," Alexandria said. Carter got to his feet and helped her up, then led her in a slow waltz through the roses. After a gentle spin, he kissed her, and more petals fell from the sky around them. They stayed in the roses and soft light for another hour before heading back inside, leaving the giant robot to clean up behind them.

CHAPTER THIRTY-THREE

True to his word, Dr. Vile kept the superheroes busy with a barrage of potential train wrecks and a prison break, while Valentine went dress shopping.

After bringing regular business to a screeching halt with her arrival, Valentine had little trouble convincing the workers to help her find a dress. Minutes later, reporters started showing up, asking Valentine questions and giving their opinions on the dresses. She got her wish, and their engagement made every major headline.

Great anticipation led to the wedding itself, the date of which was kept secret until, suddenly, photographers and news reporters, a priest, and Mr. Greys, were all abducted to a large and prominent local cathedral. Dr. Vile's robots battled off the heroes outside, while Dr. Vile and Valentine, under their true names of Carter and Alexandria, were married by the captive priest, and rode away to their honeymoon in a flying car.

After that, things quieted down a great deal, with only a few minor heists and battles with heroes, nothing to make the front page at this point. Nothing, at least, until once again they raided IKEA, this time ripping an entire nursery section from the store with their giant robot.

Every major news station went wild with the news that Dr. Vile and Valentine were expecting a baby. Valentine disappeared from the public eye during this time, and Dr. Vile was pestered at every heist for word of the baby. He kept quiet about it, however, saying that this particular event would be a private one, and that the reporters and heroes would, sadly, not be invited.

Dr. Vile then set up a small but comfortable hospital setting for Valentine in what had previously been a secret lab that one of his allies was no longer using. With a few recommendations and after carefully hacking, checking, and altering the schedules of several prominent gynecologists and doctors, he abducted what he felt to be the perfect staff of medical professionals and swore them to secrecy. It was there, in the redecorated lab and under the care of these well-compensated captives, that the baby was born, healthy and happy, with no complications. They named the baby, their son, Skylar.

Carter took off his helmet and held Skylar in his arms, beaming at him.

"Well, he got more from you than from me," he said, "though that's probably for the better."

"I think it's a bit early to tell," Alexandria said with a smile.

"I don't know, he's definitely got your ears," said Carter with a slight grin. "Look how tiny he is, is he supposed to be this small?"

"He's a baby, babies are tiny, Carter," Alexandria said.

"Well, he's very tiny," said Carter.

The doctors assured him that Skylar was perfectly normal, healthy size, and shortly afterward they were returned to their homes by the giant robot.

"I was talking to my dad," said Carter once they were gone. "He said he can arrange for a family doctor for Skylar. I figure that'll be easier than abducting doctors every time he needs a check-up."

"That's good," Alexandria said. "That would be a lot of abductions."

"No kidding," said Carter. "He's also agreed to watch Skylar while you and I are working."

"What would we ever do without your father?" Alexandria asked with a smile.

"I don't know, start a villain daycare with the others?" said Carter, pretending to think deeply about the idea. "Though I don't know if I'd quite trust them with our baby."

"Hm, me either," Alexandria said. "I like this way better."

"Yeah," said Carter. "Let's get you two home before one of the doctors gets brave and tells the police where we are."

"Good idea," Alexandria said. "Let's go home."

CHAPTER THIRTY-FOUR

Once again, the villainous activity decreased, with no more than one heist a week while Dr. Vile and Valentine stayed home as a family, each taking turns sleeping and taking care of Skylar, and just enjoying time together. After just a few weeks, Carter worked to create a scanner that would detect Skylar's health in various different measurements, which he used rather frequently, proving himself to be a very anxious but dedicated father.

As predicted, Skylar took after his mother. He had light blond hair, and his eyes soon darkened to a rusty brown, nearly matching the orange of his own energy powers. He developed his powers much earlier than either of his parents, the first sign of them showing up not long after he learned to walk.

With the constant fussing of his father, little amused Skylar more than to make his dad look for him in the enormous house. He hid in any crawlspace he could find, frequently given away by his giggling. Even so, Skylar was also soon surprised to find that his dad quickly developed what he called "psychic tracking powers," which was actually just a tracking device that Carter put in his jumpers.

By the time Skylar was four, his powers had grown to be rather unpredictable.

"Carter, I think it's time I start teaching Skylar how to control his powers," Alexandria said one day, after putting Skylar to bed.

"I'd disagree, but..." Carter glanced at the singed sleeves of one of Skylar's jumpers, which was lying in the trash. "I think you're right."

"Of course I'm right," Alexandria said with a smile. "And his powers are pretty harmless for now, better he can control them before he makes a real mess of something, right?"

"Right," said Carter. "Though maybe let's focus on how to keep it in check before getting into how to shoot things, yeah? I mean, just because he knows what he's doing won't necessarily mean he has good judgment. He's four."

"Oh, definitely," Alexandria agreed. "No shooting for a good while."

"I can set up a practice room," said Carter. He sighed. "I probably won't be much help in the lessons, though."

"Probably not," Alexandria said, then paused. "In fact….it might be better if you weren't there for the lessons."

Carter nodded dejectedly. "Yeah… I know I tend to get a little… overprotective at times."

"Yes, you do," Alexandria agreed, then smiled. "Don't worry, though, before you know it basic training will be over, then you two can have fun."

"Yeah," said Carter, smiling. "Well, I'll get started on that room, then. Maybe when you're done with basic training, we can raid IKEA again and make it a playroom."

"Sounds fun," Alexandria said, then yawned. "For now, time for sleep."

"Right, sleep," said Carter sheepishly. "Maybe I can get some blueprints written up first? Just rough sketches."

"Suit yourself," Alexandria said, pulling the blankets up around herself. "Goodnight."

He kissed her forehead. "Goodnight."

It wasn't long before Carter had the training room set up, and Alexandria began her lessons with Skylar. Skylar thought it was a great adventure, and they only had a few days of increased incidents before the lessons started helping.

A few weeks passed, and they fell into a comfortable routine. Carter had taken to working in a room just down the hall during the lessons, usually planning the logistics of the next heist.

That was where he was when he heard Skylar cry out, scared.

"Mommy? Mommy!" Skylar cried. "Daddy, help!"

Carter came stumbling out of his workroom and bolted into the practice room with a fire extinguisher in hand. Skylar stood in the middle of the room, next to Alexandria, who lay on the floor, unconscious. Skylar ran over to Carter when he came in, hugging his leg and crying. Carter dropped the extinguisher and picked up Skylar, stopping to kneel by Alexandria and try to wake her. Alexandria's pulse was almost nonexistent, her skin pale and clammy, and her breathing shallow.

"Okay, okay, um, stay here with Mommy, tap her shoulder to keep trying to wake her up," said Carter, showing Skylar how to tap Valentine with his hand. "Just tap it like that until I get back, okay? I'll get a doctor and she'll be alright."

Skylar nodded, his sobs evolving into sharp hiccups. Carter gave him a kiss on the forehead, then took off running to his hovercraft.

He rode straight to the nearest hospital, and a few minutes later he returned with a pair of doctors he'd snatched from the emergency ward, bringing them straight back to Alexandria.

Carter picked up Skylar and comforted him while the doctors worked, examining Alexandria and asking the occasional question of Carter and Skylar about what had happened. After what seemed like an eternity to Carter, but was only a few brief minutes, one of the doctors came over to him.

"We think we've identified the problem," he said. "From what we can tell, she likely has a blood clot cutting off circulation to her brain. We'll need an IV and this," he jotted down the name of a medicine and handed it to Carter, "to do anything. Time is of the essence, every minute heightens the risk of permanent brain damage."

"Okay, I'll get it, just… do what you can until I get back," said Carter, and he took off again to his hovercraft, headed back to the hospital.

As he neared the hospital, he was suddenly sideswiped by a massive sandblast. Gloria- or Desert Gust as she was now called- was close behind, wrapping him in a tight whirlwind.

"Gust!" Dr. Vile cried out. "Let me go, I don't have time for this!"

"Well I have plenty of time," Gust said, shoving him to the side with another blast.

A blast of fire hit him in the stomach as he tried to fight free of the sand and fried the machinery lining his suit along the stomach and chest. Dr. Vile's hovercraft fell out away from under him, then swooped back up to try and hit Gust from behind, while Dr. Vile used what was still working in his suit to hover and lower himself to the ground. He squinted against the sand, trying to find Emilia, now called Ember.

The hovercraft was diverted as Gust and Scuba combined their energy to send it off-course, intensifying the whirlwind. Dr. Vile coughed violently as the sand made it into his helmet, and he shot blasts of electricity at random, trying frantically to hit them, to stop the wind. He hit one of Mori's doubles, now named the Thirteenth. Another double came from behind and worked to get Dr. Vile's helmet off, only managing to do so after another blast from Ember fried the circuits.

"Stop!" Dr. Vile cried again.

"We don't take orders from you," Gust said. "Or even suggestions." Another blast of fire took out the working gears on his right leg and he fell to his knees. He gave a loud, angry cry and blasted them all with a powerful charge of electricity. They stumbled back, but only slightly.

Scuba tackled him to stop the electric charge, and soon several doubles were helping him restrain Dr. Vile. Gust kept up a swirling perimeter.

"Let me go, please," Dr. Vile begged. "I need supplies, Valentine is dying!"

"We've heard," Gust said coldly. "Don't worry, we'll take care of her while you're in prison. What's left, anyway."

There was a low rumble, then the air exploded with electricity, stunning Scuba off of Dr. Vile's back. Dr. Vile stood, and with a surprising and sudden amount of strength, he fought back with his bare hands. He winded Scuba with a hard kick to the stomach and hit Ember with an elbow to the face. He blasted Mori until all of his doubles disappeared, and he threw Gust directly into the still flaming Ember. He leaped up into the air and his hovercraft swept under him, carrying him to crash through the hospital, grab what he could, and shoot off back to the hideout in a mad race against the heroes.

By the time the heroes had regrouped, Dr. Vile was long gone.

CHAPTER THIRTY-FIVE

When Carter made it back to the hideout, he activated force fields and barricades around the house with a voice command, not stopping as he rushed the medication to the doctors. He barged into the practice room, holding out the IVs and the medication.

"I got them," he said breathlessly. "Now please, save her."

When he entered the room, the doctors froze, still kneeling over Alexandria. Their expressions were grim. One of them slowly shook his head.

"I'm sorry...."

Carter's face paled. "No..."

"She's gone," the doctor said. "There was nothing we could do."

Carter fell to his knees, his bad leg giving out and his other leg too shaky to support him now. Tears flooded his eyes and his breathing grew ragged. Then, suddenly, his expression grew dark and grim.

"You called them," he said, quietly at first. "You told the heroes where to find me."

"What?" The doctor who had spoken before exclaimed. "No, we didn't!" The other didn't speak, his expression growing more anxious.

"They knew about Valentine, they knew where I'd be. They were waiting for me," Carter growled. He looked up at them. His leg was disabled, his helmet gone, his suit was all but destroyed and his cape nearly burned entirely off, but the look he gave them struck them with terror, so much so that even his weakness seemed dangerous, like facing a wounded bear.

The doctors backed away fearfully.

"I swear," the doctor stammered, "I didn't contact anyone. Just like you said!"

"Then it's your colleague here who doesn't hold your life in high regard," said Carter. There was a faint buzz in the air, like right before a lightning strike. "My wife is dead, and if I hadn't run into those heroes, she might still be alive."

The doctors paled.

"Look, if they knew, if he told them where you were," the doctor said, "then he told them where you'd be. They'll be coming here next."

"Then you'll have someone to bury you," said Dr. Vile. He launched himself forward and took the first doctor by the throat and pumped him full of electricity to the point that he started to smoke faintly. The other doctor ran for the door as Skylar screamed, but Dr. Vile caught the man full in the back with a brilliant beam of lightning. As the doctor's body fell to the ground, so did Carter fall to his knees. He took Alexandria in his arms and sobbed, heavily and loudly.

Skylar curled up in the corner, scared and confused, and cried. Carter brought the hovercraft into the room, crashing it through the roof furthest from Skylar, and dragged Alexandria's body onto it. Then he picked up Skylar, holding him tight to his chest, before boarding the hovercraft again and flying off, away from the house, keeping low over the trees.

They made it to Mr. Greys' house, and there he pressed Skylar into Mr. Grey's arms and, without a word, took off in his hovercraft with Alexandria, leaving Mr. Greys calling out his name on the lawn. Finally, when Carter was out of sight, Mr. Greys sighed and carried Skylar inside, holding tight to the shaking boy.

Skylar could give no comprehensive explanation to his grandfather for what had happened, he didn't even know himself. He grew quiet and withdrawn during the days, unable to understand why neither of his parents would come for him. He woke up screaming from nightmares every night. One of Carter's allies contacted Mr. Greys and helped them lie low from the police while the excitement among them died out. For a full week, there was no contact from Carter, no sign of him.

Then, Dr. Vile returned, destroying the subway and everyone in the conjoined stations. Directly after, he went to the countryside where Mr. Greys and Skylar were staying.

Dr. Vile's face was cold and his eyes, once so full of kindness and cleverness, were now empty and dark. Even Mr. Greys barely recognized his son. Skylar ran up when he saw him, but stopped short at the look in his eyes.

"Daddy?" Skylar asked timidly.

"It's time to go, Skylar," said Dr. Vile. "Tell Grandpa thank you for watching you."

"Are we going home?" Skylar asked. "Is Mommy there?"

"Mommy is dead, and the heroes have taken our home," said Dr. Vile. "We're going to a new home."

"Okay," Skylar sniffled.

Dr. Vile looked at him, hesitating. "Would you... rather stay with Grandpa?"

"No," Skylar said quickly, shaking his head. "No, I want to go home with you."

Dr. Vile continued to look at him, the barest spark of warmth left in him rising to the surface. He felt overwhelmed with love for his son, his beautiful son, and he wanted to take him in his arms and never let go. At the same time, fear crept into that precious moment, and he knew he couldn't do it. He couldn't let Skylar be hurt, not like he'd let them hurt Alexandria. He couldn't take Skylar with him.

"You're going to stay here," said Dr. Vile. His throat tightened with pain. "Grandpa will take care of you. Goodbye, Skylar."

Skylar's eyes widened and he grabbed his father's arm. "No, please, Daddy, I want to go home. I want to go with you!"

Dr. Vile looked down at Skylar with tears in his eyes.

"I'm sorry, Skylar, but this is the best thing for you." He pulled his arm free and quickly went out the door and took off on his hovercraft. Skylar ran after him.

"Daddy! Please don't leave!" Skylar cried out, tears streaming down his face. Mr. Greys ran after him and caught Skylar as the hovercraft flew too far over the landscape to follow. He picked him up, holding him tight, and carried him back inside. Skylar tried to wriggle free of Mr. Grey's grip, crying hysterically.

"No, I want to go home," Skylar cried. "Put me down. I want my daddy!"

"I know, I know," said Mr. Greys softly, tears streaming from his own eyes. "I know. I'm sorry, Skylar. Your dad... your dad has decided your home is with me now."

Skylar fell against Mr. Grey's shoulder, too exhausted to struggle anymore, his sobs turned to hiccups.

"I want Mommy," he whimpered. He didn't understand what was going on, he didn't know why his father didn't want him anymore. He cried himself to sleep in Mr. Greys' arms and was carried back inside.

To Be Continued…

Coming Soon....

Skylar Greys wants to be like any normal kid, but that's impossible for the child of two of the last decade's most infamous super-villains. Eleven years after he last saw his father, Skylar now has the chance to join the ranks of young aspiring heroes at the same school that created Dr. Vile. Will Skylar be able to make a fresh start, or will his family history and his father's work pull them all into a terrible cycle?

Find out in Standardized Heroics, coming Fall 2018

Pre-order on Smashwords: https://www.smashwords.com/books/view/830474

Follow us and find out the latest for The Literary Collision

Facebook:

https://www.facebook.com/LiteraryCollision/

Twitter:

https://twitter.com/KatieandCoral

Instagram:

https://www.instagram.com/theliterarycollision/

Email:

https://mailchi.mp/a5c900eb1c4f/the-literary-collision-email-subscription

Amazon Author Page:

https://www.amazon.com/-/e/B07D6DLFLC

Smashwords Author Page

https://www.smashwords.com/profile/view/CoralElizabeth

https://www.smashwords.com/profile/view/KatherineLee

Acknowledgements

We would like to thank the amazing contributions given by our beta readers, who gave great insight during the editing stages.

We owe an abundance of thanks to Coral's father, Roy Hayward, for helping us format our book for ebook and hard copies in such a short amount of time.

We would also like to thank Coral's cousin (first cousin once removed? Not sure, we're related somehow!) Christopher, who cast the shadow for the picture on the back cover of our hard copy (and will be featured in the front cover of our upcoming sequel: Standardized Heroics.)

We'd like to thank the American Fork Rec Center for allowing us to use their lockers to take pictures for our lovely front cover. We couldn't have asked for a better color scheme to model our pink cape.

We're very grateful to Coral's sister, Sarah Hayward, for doing basically all of the sewing for the cape on our cover, and for her other artistic contributions to the process.

We're forever grateful to the writing workshop group, Nine Bridges, in Lehi, for giving us their valuable feedback. Scuba would not be the man he is today without them.

We extend our eternal gratitude to Canva.com, for being the amazing website that allowed us to make our gorgeous cover (for free!)

We'd like to thank Grammarly for helping us curtail our abundance of commas and for whoever invented ctrl+f, for allowing us to find and vanquish excessively used words.

Coral would like to thank JK Rowling for writing Harry Potter and inspiring her to become a writer when she was six, and Katie would like to thank Kim Possible and Spy Kids for inspiring her to become a child super-spy, which later evolved into her writing career.

The Class Villain

About the Authors

Katherine Lee
As written by Coral Elizabeth

Katherine Lee was born in the year 1995, on a Friday (apparently, I wasn't there,) and the world has never been the same. It has been considerably stranger. She is the second of six children, born an raised in American Fork Utah.

Her love of writing started at a young age, and her childhood never had a dull moment. That's putting it mildly, to say the least. From staring contests with snakes to an intense mistrust of costumed adults, I could go on for days with funny anecdotes. I will refrain, however.

Katherine's place on the autism spectrum has always given her a unique way of seeing the world. This never held her back, however, and she enjoyed years in the gifted program in elementary school. Some of her fondest memories of that time include mummifying chickens and reading every book she could get her hands on.

Katherine had a variety of pets growing up, including mice, bunnies and cats, but sadly her families allergies made most of these short lived. She looks forward to adopting two kittens when she moves to Salt Lake City soon to room with me.

I became friends with Katherine in Junior High and we have stayed friends ever since. Katherine enjoyed sewing and cooking classes in school, and writing stories nonstop outside of it.

After High School graduation, Katherine went on to earn a Bachelors degree of creative writing with a minor in film to prepare for the day when our writing partnership would take over the world.

Coral Elizabeth
As written by Katherine Lee

Coral Elizabeth was overly articulate from a young age, full of vocabulary words found in books that miffed teachers and was applauded by her parents. Homeschooled and raised in Tennessee, she learned early on to work hard, follow rules, and to dig in her heels when someone tells her to do something she shouldn't. Those ideals came with her to Utah when her family moved here, and are still with her to this day.

Coral is a woman of many talents, having played the bassoon and bass clarinet for the American Fork High School Marching Band, learned to speak German, learned Latin, now speaks Spanish, is a bargain-shopping extraordinaire, and continues to self-study her way into other fields and talents, including marketing, child care, and entrepreneurship. She writes religious poetry (some in Spanish) and continues to drive herself forward in becoming a published author of sci fi and fantasy novels.

In addition to her intelligence and talent, hard work and determination are equally defining characteristics of Coral. She twisted her ankle during practice at one point, then continued to march on it until she twisted again and was ordered off the field. During her first semester of college, she worked to pay for her own housing and tuition, took all the hardest classes possible for your first year (including Anthropology,) and still spent hours upon hours writing stories with me. After that, she took a brief break (though not from working) and earned money to pay her way through an 18-month, Spanish speaking service mission for the Church of Jesus Christ of Latter-Day Saints, which she served in Chicago. From her time there, she gained a greater appreciation for Latin-American culture and language, and still randomly will speak Spanish at me to this day.

Family and service are extremely important to Coral, as she has more siblings than I can remember off the top of my head. She had at least six to start with, possibly more, and then her family adopted enough to nearly double that number, determined to take in sibling groups, and are expecting to adopt more soon. She knows and loves each and every one of her siblings, despite knowing some for barely a year or two now, and proceeded to take it upon herself to create her own charity to raise money to help buy shoes and other amenities for children admitted into the foster care system without them.

Coral's pet peeves include people mispronouncing her name (pronunciations such as Corral and Carol plague her constantly,) being cold, and (though I think I'm wearing her down on this) cats. She loves dogs, the color orange, Tennessee, southern stuff, fandoms, sweaters, good movies, giant bean bag chairs, cosplay, and cooking. She currently lives in Utah, working hard to support her charity, novel writing, and continued college education, and soon hopes to move to Salt Lake City to earn a Marketing degree and continue her authorship with me and a yet to be adopted dog.

Coral Elizabeth and Katherine Lee

23670225R00089

Made in the USA
Columbia, SC
11 August 2018